DANA LECHEMINANT

Kiss ME IF YOU Can

a sweet rom com novella

ISBN: 978-1-951753-21-4

Author's Note

THE LOVE IN SUN City series can be read in any order, as stand-alones or together. Writing this series has been such a fun experience for me because the four stories (as well as this novella) all overlap and share scenes over the course of a month. Not only did I get to discover the stories, but I also got to discover them *at the same time*. It was a cool experiment to see how this type of project would work, and hopefully it gets you excited for the other stories as you read this one. I've added dates to each book to help you keep track of shared events, if you so desire. :)

Enjoy your time with the Briggs siblings (and Jake) as they simultaneously (and quickly) fall madly in love!

– Dana

Chapter One

Jake

June 27

Whoever invented neckties should be thrown in jail. I tug at the stupid thing around my neck, trying to get some freedom from the silk contraption, but Agent Fields gives me a glare from the other side of the large, circular fountain between us, where he's pretending to read a newspaper on the bench opposite from mine. *A newspaper.* If he's trying to blend in, he's doing a worse job than me.

A male voice crackles in my ear, full of static and almost too choppy to understand. "Relax, Mr. Moody. The contact will be here any moment."

"You clearly don't know what helps me relax," I grumble back. "And don't call me that."

"It's your name. Please stop talking, Mr. Moody."

I suppose I do look like I'm talking to myself as I sit on this bench alone, but that doesn't stop me from continuing my observably one-sided conversation. "You know you could boost the signal of these earpieces if you used satellites over cell towers, right? You're not even that far away, and I can barely hear you."

"Mr. Moody, please—"

"Plus, I'm pretty sure he'll be checking for wires as soon as he shows up," I continue, while Fields looks ready to murder me as he continues to glare over his newspaper. I'm pretty sure he's contemplating turning off his earpiece so he doesn't have to keep listening to my conversation with the man in the van whose name I've already forgotten. "I'm sure you're aware that technology has evolved past using actual wires. This thing tickles like you wouldn't believe." And the wire taped to my chest is nothing compared to the tie that feels like a shiny red noose around my neck.

I don't know why I'm poking this particular bear. It's probably a bad idea to mess with the FBI, but I really expected them to be more competent than this. The out-of-date equipment is putting me on edge.

"Mr. Moody, if you don't stop talking, I could have you arrested for obstruction of justice."

I slouch against the back of the park bench, tugging at my tie again because it really does feel like it's strangling me. I haven't worn a suit since my high school graduation nine years ago, and this getup is giving me horrible flashbacks of my teenage years. Not a time I would like to relive.

"Technically," I mutter, glancing around the sunny, people-filled park, "I'm not obstructing anything. The contact isn't anywhere in sight, and the only reason I'm here is because I'm the one who uncovered his operation and *you guys* aren't smart enough to talk to him. Arrest me if you want, but that will only let this guy get away. Your choice."

Fields looks like he's about to give up his post and come strangle me himself, so I give him a little wave and tug my tie extra loose, knowing he can't do anything about it.

My earpiece is silent, which means I've either angered the man in the van enough for him to abort the operation, or he knows I'm right. The *only* reason I agreed to this stupid meeting is because there's a limited window of opportunity to catch this guy. Frank Hadley has been slowly building a digital battering ram that breaks through even the toughest firewalls in minutes, and his targeted smash and grabs against innocents caught my attention a couple of weeks ago. He's next to impossible to track until he's already struck, but my team of cyber security experts managed to find a way to contact him and set up a meeting for me under the pretext of wanting to join forces as a fellow hacker.

I hate that word. *Hacker*. It calls to mind cheap movie gimmicks of clacking keyboards and scrolling code and minimizes the intelligence it takes to understand programming at such a deep level. Hacking is taking a dull hatchet to a block of wet wood, not delicately dancing with the nuances of technology.

But I digress. Hadley miraculously agreed to meet me while he's in New Mexico for a day before he disappears into the wind. I alerted the FBI so I could let someone else handle the physical stuff while I worked to destroy his invasive program, but no. They begged me to make the actual contact, so here I am.

In a suit.

For the record, hackers don't wear suits. We wear whatever we please because there's no point in being uncomfortable. Unfortunately, the feds weren't open to suggestions.

Also for the record, I am *not* a hacker. I just happen to have a lot of skills that may or may not translate into the hacking world. We don't have to talk about the things I did in my youth. That doesn't count.

"We may have the target in sight," a female voice says over the earpiece. "Everyone on high alert. Suspect may be armed."

Fields stiffens in his seat, his hands going tight around the newspaper.

I stay where I am, trying not to look suspicious as I glance around the park. There are dozens of people within a hundred yards of me, and I wouldn't say any of them look shifty. I doubt my contact is the woman playing frisbee golf with her friend or the guy pacing while talking on his phone. Honestly, everyone in this park looks like a normal human enjoying a perfect summer day.

Hadley said he would know me when he saw me, though I haven't figured out how. I don't exist on the internet and I don't own a cell phone, so I'm next to untraceable. Either he's way better at his job than I am—unlikely but possible—or he knows

I'm going to be surrounded by field agents. There's a high chance Hadley has heard my name, and his curiosity is the only thing that brought him out today.

"Where's he coming from?" I ask, trying not to move my mouth.

No one responds, though Fields has a distant look in his eyes, like he's listening to something I'm not hearing. Stupid faulty earpiece... I *really* don't like being kept out of the loop when I'm the sitting duck in a tie. This is why I didn't want to be a part of this. This is why I don't generally trust the government. I've seen too many downfalls and not enough positives, and they're really not helping their case right now by leaving me in the dark.

Fields stands, looking over at me while tucking a hand in his jacket, where his shoulder holster holds his gun. The murderous look hasn't left his eyes. Nor has his focus shifted away from me. He narrows his eyes, and cold dread settles in my stomach.

I sit up straight. He's not going to shoot me, is he? Why would he? I'm on *their* side.

"Abort! We've been made!" The radio turns to static, but three disjointed words make it through the noise: "Take. Moody. Out."

The instant I see Fields's pistol glistening in the sun and pointed right at me, I bolt. A gunshot echoes behind me. People scream. Someone shouts my name but I don't stop running. I dodge trees, trying to avoid the congested paths so there's no one caught in the crosshairs. Only when I've crossed half the park do I glance back without slowing down.

I don't see anyone hot on my heels, but that doesn't mean I'm safe. I have to—

I collide with something hard, grunting as pain radiates through me on impact. Whatever I hit—whoever—they fall with me. We both tumble through some shrubs and down a hidden hill in a tangle of limbs until we land in a heap at the bottom of a heavily foliaged ravine.

I groan, struggling to free myself so I can keep running. That wasn't fun. At all. "Sorry."

The woman beneath me doesn't move, her blonde hair obscuring her face.

I swear, forcing myself to ignore my own pain as I check her for injuries. "Miss? Can you hear me?"

My heart stops for a fleeting moment when I only find one leg, thinking the other is bent beneath her or something and definitely broken, until I realize the end of her thigh doesn't continue downward. I breathe a sigh of relief. "Oh, good. It's just missing."

"Most people don't see that as a good thing."

My eyes snap to her face to find her glaring at me. "You're okay."

She narrows her bright blue eyes. "No thanks to you. Were you a linebacker in a past life?"

I can't stop the single laugh that rushes out of me. This is not the time for laughing! "Why couldn't I be a linebacker now?"

Her gaze slides down my body as she lifts her head to get a better view. "Uh, because you probably weigh a buck fifty? Which is still more than I want on top of me, thank you very much." She shoves her hands into my chest with impressive strength, pushing me to the side to free herself.

Yeah, I'm not a big guy. I do yoga before bed and occasionally hit the gym if I'm feeling particularly frustrated. I care more about flexibility and health than strength. Still, her assessment stings. Why this matters when I was almost executed just now, I have no idea.

"I hit you pretty hard," I mumble, brushing leaves and dirt from my sleeves as I try to calm my heart rate so I can think clearly and figure out my next move. "Sorry about that."

As she sits up, she looks through the vines and weeds around her as if searching for something. "Aha," she says and picks up a phone. Then her eyes lift to the hill we just tumbled down. "You wouldn't happen to see my leg up there anywhere, would you? I might need that if I'm going to—"

I grab her, wrapping my palm over her mouth and dragging her against my chest as I press myself into the side of the hill to hide.

Three men, none of them familiar, just appeared at the top with frantic looks in their eyes, and I'm not keen to be murdered today. Whether they're FBI or with Hadley, they're going to be out to get me.

"Stay quiet," I hiss to my sudden captive, "and I'll make sure you live through this."

Chapter Two
Isla

GO TO SUN CITY, they said. *It will be fun*, they said.

What they didn't say was how likely I would get tackled and then kidnapped by a madman in a suit that wasn't made for him, so I think they need to change the city slogan from "where the sun never stops" to "make sure you bring a Taser and a change of clothes." And here I thought today was going to be a great day.

If I hadn't lost my prosthesis in the tumble down the hill, I would be more inclined to try to fight my way out of this, but what am I going to do if I get out of his hold? Crawl away? Hop to freedom? He'd probably kill me before I got two yards along the ravine.

I try to twist enough to see what he's doing, maybe figure out why we're just sitting here, but he holds me too tight. It looks like he's looking up the hill where we came from, but beyond that I've got nothing.

Nothing but a ruined outfit and my own wits, which seem to have abandoned me the moment I got tackled but are slowly making their way back. Why am I just sitting here waiting? I have my phone in my hand, and all I have to do is make a call.

Trying not to move, I slowly shift my phone to get to the fingerprint lock, doing my best to keep it out of sight of my captor.

Darn. My hands are too dirty, and it won't take my thumbprint. Why did I have to make my pattern lock so complicated? With no way to hold my phone in my other hand, I have to awkwardly try to reach all the dots with my tiny thumb. Curse my impulsive self for buying the latest and greatest phone! This thing is a brick, and I should have known I would one day only have use of one hand.

I remember when phones were being designed smaller and smaller, and then smartphones happened and now they just keep getting bigger again. In a few years, we'll all be carrying tablets around unless they get around to inventing holographic screens.

Finally I get through the lock screen, but now I'm not sure what I can actually do. I could call the police, but there's nothing I can say with my captor's hand pressed over my mouth. I can text my brother-in-law? But sending a text is risky and might take too long. I've sent too many "emergency" texts to Cam for him to properly interpret "911" if I try that. Same with "help" or any form of telling him I'm in danger.

He says I'm dramatic. He's right. No matter what I send him, this is going to be a "boy who cried wolf" situation. Yay. Besides, he's two hours away in Diamond Springs, so even if he came it wouldn't help me much in the immediate.

I don't think anyone can help me except myself.

A sigh escapes me before I can hold it back.

The poorly dressed criminal tightens his hold. "I'm sorry. You'll thank me someday."

"Why would I thank you for holding me hostage?" I ask, but it sounds like a bunch of muffled nonsense against his hand.

His thumb presses more firmly against my cheek, and I struggle uselessly for a few seconds. My body is starting to ache in places I didn't know it could ache, and his hand is way too soft for a kidnapper. Just like how he smells far too good for a bad guy. What sort of criminal smells like eucalyptus and lemon?

He lets out a breath into my hair that almost sounds like a sigh of relief. "They're finally gone. I'm going to let you go, but you have to promise not to scream or anything, okay? That will just bring them back."

Why would I promise something like that?

In the strangest move I've ever seen, he wraps one leg around me and shifts, his shoulder twisting in a way it shouldn't as he maneuvers himself so he's straddling over me instead of beneath me, all without moving his hand from my mouth.

What, is he some sort of boneless demon? His arm shouldn't be able to do that.

He chuckles, his gaze dropping down to his elbow. "Double jointed." Then he swaps hands so he's no longer holding me so bizarrely. "Promise not to make a sound?"

I shake my head, glaring at him.

His expression softens. "Please? I really don't want to get shot, and I'm assuming you don't either. But if that's what you want, scream to your heart's content but give me a thirty-second head start."

He grins sheepishly, revealing a single deep dimple on his right side. Curse that dimple! Bad guys don't have dimples, so now my brain is choosing to trust him. This is going to bite me in the butt, isn't it? But what choice do I have?

I roll my eyes, which he must interpret as my reluctant agreement because he slowly lifts his hand from my mouth, watching me carefully for any sign that I might change my mind. Once I've proven that I'm not going to scream—still up for debate—he shifts away from me to let me sit up again.

"Thank you," he says, right as he sheds his suit coat. The tie comes off next, and when he starts unbuttoning his shirt, my panic returns.

"Oh, no you don't, buddy," I growl, grabbing the nearest rock and holding it up, ready to throw it at him the second he makes a move.

He freezes, eyes on the rock and his hands in the air. "Easy," he says. "I'm not going to do anything to you." One hand returns to his buttons, though he keeps the other in the air as if to prove he's not going to come at me.

When he reveals a wire taped to his surprisingly defined chest, my mouth gapes open. "Oh my gosh, are you a narc?"

He frowns. "A what?"

"You know, like a CI? Criminal informant? Bad guy forced into working for the good guys?"

As he peels the wire from his skin, bringing with it a little box that must hold the recording device, he keeps looking at me like I'm speaking nonsense. "You know the term is *Confidential* Informant, right?"

That can't be right. "No, it's criminal. Because it's always bad guys. Criminals. Who inform."

He laughs again before tossing the device into the little stream at the bottom of the ravine. (Thank goodness we didn't land in the stream. I am—was—having way too good of a hair day for that.) "It's *confidential* because their information generally isn't used against them."

Okay, the longer I look at this guy, the more I think my brain might be right about him. There's nothing sinister about his features or his body language as he buttons his shirt back up, and in any other circumstance I would consider him to be downright cute. He's got the boy-next-door look to him, with that little dimple and thick brown hair that has no product or style whatsoever. It's like he doesn't know what to do with it so he just lets it flop on his forehead and do whatever it wants.

And he has kind eyes. They're a soft shade of green I've never seen before, and they really do make him look nice and approachable.

I mentally slap myself. *This guy held you against your will, Isla!* I really shouldn't need that reminder, but apparently I do. And all because he has a pretty face.

Why does this always happen to me?

As he gets to his feet, his focus on the top of the hill, I decide to be brave.

"Who's chasing you?"

"That's a good question," he mutters. "I probably shouldn't stay here and find out. Do you need..." He glances down at my legs and then looks back up the hill where we came. "You said your, uh, leg might be up there?"

I roll my eyes. Leg, liner, sock—I lost it all in the fall. "Well, I was wearing it when you crashed into me, and now I'm not. You do the math." I hop up to my foot, determined to get my prosthesis myself if I have to. I wobble when a sharp pain in my knee tells me I am more injured than I realized. A glance down reveals multiple cuts and bruises on my bare skin because I wore a mini skirt today. *Ouch.*

At least I wore sneakers instead of heels like I usually do. Balancing on one heel is not for the faint of heart.

"Here," my kidnapper says, holding out his arm. "If you want help."

Most guys assume I'm incapable of getting myself around because I'm the poor girl who lost her leg as a kid, and they don't offer me a choice when it comes to helping me. Granted, I usually gladly take the help because I don't like hopping, especially when I'm wearing a more low-cut top like today and a bra that is not nearly supportive enough for that sort of thing. But I appreciate the choice.

I tuck my arm through his, getting another whiff of his clean scent. "Thanks."

A shout overhead pulls our attention up the hill, and my kidnapper curses under his breath when a man in a suit runs past the edge of the ravine. But not like a full run. It was more of a searching run, like there's a good chance he'll come back this way in a second.

"Here are the options," my dimpled criminal says, grimacing when he looks at me. "I can leave you here and let you get yourself out of the ravine and hopefully to your leg."

I wrinkle my nose. That hill is looking rather daunting. "Or?"

He twists and crouches just a bit, offering his back to me. "Or I can take you with me on my back, hoping you have a car or something, and you can help me find a place to hide and figure out what went wrong up there."

I know which option has the more likely outcome of me being murdered. I also know that I've already fallen down that ravine wall, and I don't especially want to climb back up on my own. My keys are around my neck, so I *could* get us out of here. But can I trust him?

Groaning, I hop onto the guy's back and pray Cam never hears about any of this. Or my sister, for that matter. Kailani would kill me for trusting a stranger who is clearly being chased by someone.

But dimple! My gut wants me to trust this guy, so I'm going to trust him. "My car is that way. I'm Isla, by the way."

He hesitates, glancing back up the hill before tucking his hands under my thighs. "I'm Jake."

Chapter Three
Jake

I GUESS I'M A kidnapper now? That's the only thing I can think as I drive Isla's car all over Sun City, trying to figure out the best place for me to go. I don't want to risk going home, even if my apartment is registered under a fake name, and I especially can't go to the office because my company is *not* listed under a fake name. I probably need to find a way to alert my team that the FBI is going to be showing up at some point, if they haven't already, but I've made it so no one can get through to my company unless they've been vetted and set up from the inside.

Why did I have to put up such strong security?

Regardless, I need to stop driving around willy-nilly before Isla thinks I'm completely out of my depth, even though I am. I already made a fool of myself by weaving in and out of the stream that ran through the ravine, at least until Isla said I was just wasting time and getting my socks wet.

She was weirdly helpful by keeping an eye out from my back while I crept to her car in an empty and obscure part of the park, but I'm not sure I can trust that she won't cause problems. I need to make sure she only sees confidence instead of weaknesses she can exploit. I'm not off to a good start.

"Where are we going?" she asks before I can figure out a plan of action.

I glance at her. "It's better if you don't know."

"That's not sketchy at all." She rolls her eyes and brushes a hand over her skirt, pulling my attention to her legs.

They're all torn up, especially the one that ends mid-thigh, and I'm pretty sure that's going to cause problems if she tries to wear her prosthesis. That's my fault. Not only did I lose her leg, but even if we go back and get it, she's not going to be able to wear it.

"Sorry," I mutter, pulling my eyes away from her fair skin. Probably not a good idea to keep staring at her legs.

"Sorry for staring?" she replies, and there's plenty of snark in her voice.

It almost brings a smile out of me. "I meant I'm sorry for hurting you, but I guess I should apologize for staring as well. I wasn't looking at..." I swallow, knowing I'm likely to offend her if I put this the wrong way. "I was looking at your injuries. You need to get them clean."

"So you weren't looking at my stump like it's a train wreck and you just can't look away?"

No, but she's not going to believe me. "Will you let me help you?" I pull into the parking lot of a drugstore anyway, even if it's probably a bad idea to stop. I can't be sure that no one saw me leaving the park with Isla, even if I haven't seen any sign of a tail, but I'm not about to let Isla be at risk of infection when she let me use her car.

She sighs as if this is the most inconvenient thing to ever happen to her. It probably is. "Fine. But you're going to walk in there looking like that?"

I glance down, noticing for the first time the rips and tears in my suit pants. Not to mention the dirt. My shirt is clean—the jacket took the brunt of the fall—but that doesn't necessarily do me much good. "Do I have a choice?"

She shrugs. "I might have some sweatpants or something in the trunk."

"Do they say 'juicy' on the rear end?"

To my surprise, she actually laughs a little at that. "No, but they're definitely designed for women." She lifts an eyebrow. "You don't exactly have the curves to fill them in right, but they might be better than what you're wearing now."

I get the sense that she's judging more than just the damage. Hitting the button to open the trunk, I step out and rummage through the surprising number of clothing items back there before climbing into the backseat so I can change.

"This suit isn't mine," I tell her as I struggle out of the slacks, though I don't really care what she thinks of me. "I borrowed it from the FBI." Why in the world did I just tell her that?

"How exactly does someone borrow clothes from the FBI?"

"It's pretty easy when they force you to be the bait for a dangerous cyber criminal."

"Is that what you were doing at the park?"

Once I've managed to get into the sky blue sweatpants, I lean forward, resting an arm on the back of the driver's seat, and give her a smirk. I'm guessing she responds better to humor than seriousness, and I need to use every advantage I've got. "Wasn't it obvious?"

She narrows her eyes. "So, if you were working with the FBI, why did you run?"

I unbutton my shirt so I can put on the t-shirt I found in the trunk as well. "Turns out that's the natural response to getting a gun pointed at you."

"Who was pointing the gun? The criminal?"

I frown. I haven't been able to stop thinking about it. "The agent. I don't know why. Something must have gone wrong with the meetup, and suddenly he's trying to shoot me." It had to have been a setup, not just to catch Hadley but to catch me too. Two birds, one stone. Final justice for the one who got away. "But I didn't do anything wrong." *Today.*

Isla scoffs, raising an eyebrow at me. "And I should believe you because...?"

"Because I'm telling the truth." Slipping my shoes back on, I open the door but pause, looking back at her. "If you're gone when

I come back out, I'll understand. I don't expect you to help me or even believe me, and you've already done more than I can thank you for."

I don't wait for her to respond. It'll be better if I give her every opportunity to make her own choices, even if I hope she doesn't leave me stranded at a CVS on the other side of town from my apartment. There's nothing over here that can help me, though I'm honestly not sure if anything can help me in the first place.

In general, people can't hide from the FBI for long. They found me once; they'll find me again.

The CVS is pretty much empty as I step inside, some sort of pop song playing on the radio overhead while the girl behind the counter scrolls through her phone without looking up. There's an older gentleman browsing the fungal creams, but beyond that I pretty much have the store to myself.

That's an unexpected blessing.

Gathering up as many first aid supplies as I can without taking too much time, I snag a bag of trail mix as well and head to the counter, not willing to spend more time than I need to.

"Find everything you need?" the girl asks without looking up.

"Yep. All good."

She's giving off some kind of vibe that doesn't fully fit with her disinterested exterior, like there's an undercurrent of some nervousness just beneath the surface. I glance at her unlocked phone sitting on the counter as she rings me up, curious about what she was looking at, and nearly swear when I see a picture of my face above a headline that reads, *Known cyber terrorist loose in Sun City.*

Apparently the FBI haven't wasted any time.

"Would you like to sign up for our rewards program?" the girl asks as she scans the last item and picks up the cash I put on the counter.

"Not today, thank you."

"Have a great..." She looks up, halfway through handing my bag to me, and then glances down at her phone. Back at me. Back at her phone.

"You too," I say, snatching the bag and heading for the door.

"Hey!"

I ignore her, keeping my eyes fixed ahead and praying Isla didn't drive off without me.

By some miracle, she's still in the parking lot, though she's moved to the driver's seat and seems to be watching me with a lot more suspicion in her expression than before. I shouldn't have left her alone with her phone and all its access to the internet, but I wasn't about to steal it from her.

That was a mistake.

I grab the passenger door handle, only to find it locked, and tension fills my body as I glance back at the drugstore, though it's not like I expect the girl to come after me. I *do* expect her to call the police, and that means I only have a few minutes before this place is crawling with cops and feds.

I meet Isla's eyes again, begging her to let me into the car, but she doesn't move. I don't blame her. Guess it's time for me to start running and hope I can find a good place to hide.

Setting the bag of supplies on the hood of the car, I nod once at Isla and then turn to figure out my best route. I should probably head behind the store and avoid the streets as much as I can, though now I'm regretting these sweatpants because they're not exactly lowkey. All the FBI will have to do is tell the public to look for the weirdo wearing blue women's sweatpants, and I'll be found in minutes.

"Hey."

I turn, surprised to see the passenger window rolled down and Isla leaning over to get a better look at me.

"Get in."

She doesn't have to tell me twice. I tug the door open and slip inside, grabbing the supplies. "Drive," I tell her. "I don't care where."

Part of me expects her to peel out of the parking lot and zoom away, but she's smart enough to know that will only draw attention to us. She keeps herself at a normal speed, using her blinker as she turns onto the road and heads south.

We're both quiet for a minute. I'm listening for police sirens, and I'm pretty sure Isla is second-guessing herself because she keeps glancing at me. Plus, she's giving off a lot of different vibes right now, like she can't decide what to think about all of this. I'm waiting for the moment she pulls over to the curb and kicks me out.

"I don't know where to go," she says after a while. "I've never been to Sun City before."

I noticed her Colorado plates, but I wasn't about to ask for more information about her. The less we know about each other, the less danger she'll be in. She's already going to be in a lot of trouble if we get caught, though I will do my best to play it off as a kidnapping, not aiding and abetting.

"We need to find somewhere quiet," I say, wishing I had any sort of plan. It's not like I've ever been on the run from the government. Not like this, anyway. "Maybe a different park?"

"As long as it doesn't have any ravines," Isla mumbles under her breath. "Shouldn't you not go somewhere public? Your face is kind of all over the news."

I point at her phone. "May I?" I need to know what I'm up against.

"Knock yourself out."

By the time Isla pulls into the lot of a fairly crowded park that is mostly made up of baseball diamonds, I've learned quite a lot about my predicament. Only one news station—Sun City's most popular station, Channel 6—has labeled me a cyber terrorist, while the rest of the stories only say the police are looking for me and I might be dangerous. I have a feeling someone tipped off Channel 6, and it wouldn't surprise me to learn Hadley is behind that one. He would have done his research, and if he realized the FBI were at the park with me, it would make sense for him to retaliate.

Still, I don't appreciate the reminder of my past, no matter how accurate.

"Does this work?" Isla asks. "I thought maybe we could sit on the bleachers and blend in with the people watching the game."

The more people that are around, the more likely I am to be recognized, but hopefully most of the people here are parents and too busy watching the Little League game to be looking up breaking news on their phones.

I nod and hand her back her phone, though I'm sorely tempted to keep it and disable anything that could be tracked. I don't think she would appreciate losing her best resource if she finally decides she shouldn't trust me.

"Is it true?" she asks, looking down at her phone.

That's a loaded question, one I don't know how to answer without risking her running away. "I'm not a bad person," I say instead. It's a lame response, but it's the only one I've got right now. "I thought you were going to leave me at CVS."

"So did I."

"Why didn't you?"

She shrugs. "I don't know. I guess I had a feeling about you."

It shouldn't, but her response makes me smile. I'm all about gut feelings and intuition, but there aren't many people who trust their own hearts anymore. It's nice to find a kindred spirit, even if it's just temporary.

I pick up the bag of supplies. "Ready?"

She studies me for a moment, and then she smiles. In this moment, everything about her is warm and welcoming, and I hope she doesn't find a reason for that to change. There's something about

Isla that makes me want to keep her around, and I have a feeling I'm not going to get through the day without her.

Chapter Four

Isla

THIS MIGHT BE THE strangest day of my life, and that's saying something. I've lived a pretty strange life.

As we climb out of the car to the sounds of cheers from the nearby baseball game, I try not to stare at Jake. It's really hard not to do. I seriously thought about driving away as soon as he disappeared inside the pharmacy, but I hate the idea of not helping someone in need. So I opened up my phone to check my messages while I waited, only to find a text from my brother-in-law, who somehow stumbled across a news story talking about what happened at the park. According to the article, Jake Moody is a dangerous cyber criminal who evaded capture and needs to be apprehended immediately.

Maybe the criminal thing is right. Jake didn't deny it. But dangerous? Looking at him, I'm pretty sure there's not a dangerous bone in his body. Even when I locked him out of the car, he didn't once glare at me or threaten or even beg me to let him in. Instead, he left the first aid stuff and was about to leave before I told him to come with me. No matter how much logic is telling me to stay away from this guy, my instinct is telling me to help him.

I tend to think my instinct is usually right. After all, my gut told me to quit school and start my own clothing line, and look at me now. I have hundreds of thousands of followers on social media, a website that consistently sells out, and a potential collaboration deal. Assuming I make it to my meeting later today...

I told Cam that I was nowhere near the park and that he didn't need to be checking up on me while I was in New Mexico, and then

I waited for Jake to return while ignoring any other texts that came through. Now I'm here, hoping my instinct is still just as sharp as it has been in the past. Otherwise, today is going to turn out a lot differently than I hoped.

"How can I help?" Jake says, nodding toward my hand where it rests on the car for balance.

I really wish I had my leg. Hopefully no one finds it and takes it before I can go back for it; those things aren't cheap. For now... "I have some crutches in the trunk," I tell him. I only make it one hop before he's at the trunk, pulling them out for me. "Thank you." Another reason why it's hard to think he might actually be a criminal. He's been nothing but kind to me since the moment we collided. But what if I'm wrong?

He must sense my hesitation because once I'm settled with my forearm crutches, he takes a step back. "We don't have to do this," he says, nodding toward the bag. "I can leave this with you and fend for myself so you don't get into any trouble."

I scoff, even though the logical side of me—a very small part—knows I should take his offer. "I have been in trouble my entire life. I'm not going to stop now. Besides, I'm squeamish around blood."

That's a lie. I'm the person who watches doctor shows with fascination and looks up injury videos on YouTube because the human body is just so interesting. I wish I had been awake when my leg was amputated; even at nine years old I would have loved to see the process. My sister, Kailani, thinks I'm crazy, but that has never stopped me. Bring on the blood and gore, baby.

Jake doesn't need to know that, though.

Pursing his lips, he looks down at my torn-up legs and then nods toward the bleachers. "Let's find a place to sit. Hopefully no one pays much attention to us, but in case they do, maybe we should—"

"Oh, I've got that covered."

Though he tilts his head, clearly curious about my unspoken plan, I keep it to myself. It'll be easier if I just do my thing.

Jake leads the way to the bleachers but pauses at the edge. There's plenty of space underneath them for us to do our thing without being the center of attention, and that would probably be better than sitting in plain sight.

"Oh my gosh, are you okay?" A woman who passes us on her way to the bleachers touches her hand to my arm, which is scraped up and dirty.

I smile and gesture to my stump, even though Jake looks ready to run beside me. "Just clumsy. You know how it is."

Just as I expected, she turns red and hurries away. Not everyone is so avoidant, but most people are. It has its perks sometimes, like now, when I know she probably won't say anything to anyone else, leaving us in peace for a little bit.

Jake grits his teeth as he settles on the ground a few feet beneath the bleachers and pulls out some alcohol wipes, though he doesn't say anything.

"Most people don't know how to treat people like me," I tell him quietly. "They either take pity on the poor little girl without a leg and think I'm incapable of anything or look at me like I'm some abomination who needs to be hidden away."

Shaking his head, he helps me settle beside him and then lifts my good leg, stretching it out across his lap. "They're wrong, Isla. Losing a limb doesn't make you less human."

"Maybe not, but it does make me different." I hiss when he touches the wipe to the first cut, and he freezes. "No, keep going. I just wasn't ready for you."

Story of the day. I came to Sun City hoping to meet up with an influencer who has repped some of the biggest brands in athletic wear and has almost a million followers because of her work to empower women. I had some time to kill before my meeting, so I found a nice-looking park and went for a walk to calm my nerves.

I certainly wasn't ready for some guy to tackle me down a hill, nor was I ready to encounter one of the nicest people I've ever met.

Can I call him nice when he sort of kidnapped me?

Regardless, I never expected to be sitting underneath metal bleachers with a decently good view of the game through the slats. It's a Little League game with a surprising number of spectators given the low skill of the players.

"So, what's your story?" Jake asks, keeping his eyes on his task as he slowly cleans my leg.

I turn back to him. "I lost my leg when I was nine. Bone cancer."

He pauses, his gaze jumping up to meet mine as his dimple makes an appearance with his smile. "That isn't what I asked."

"Oh."

"Who are you, Isla? Why are you in Sun City? Why did you decide to trust me when you have every reason not to?"

For some reason, my breath catches in my throat as he resumes his ministrations. I don't know if it's the questions that hit me, or the way his fingers are so gentle as they work their way from my ankle to my knee. Whatever it is, something is bubbling up in my belly the longer we sit here.

"I'm Isla," I say with a shrug, glad that he chuckles at my poor excuse for a joke. I'm usually a lot wittier than this, but it's been a crazy morning so far. "I was born in Hawaii, not that you'd ever guess it looking at me, and my parents adopted me when I was a baby. I'm the third oldest of ten kids—wait, eleven now—most of us adopted. I work in clothing design, though I've been focusing on athletic wear because my sister and her husband run a big, fancy gym in Diamond Springs and helped me get started by selling my stuff to their clients."

I pause when he gets to a particularly deep gouge running the length of my shin, gritting my teeth as he cleans the dirt from the wound.

Without even looking up, he reaches over and grabs my hand, giving it a squeeze as if to tell me I can squeeze right back if I need to.

Who in the world is this man?

"I'm in Sun City to meet with an influencer who might be able to help me grow my brand," I continue. "She commented on one of my posts a few weeks ago and said she loved my stuff, and when I realized she was here in New Mexico, I begged her to let me take her out to lunch and talk a collab."

Pausing again, Jake meets my eyes. "You haven't missed your meeting, have you?"

"Not yet. It's not until two."

He looks up at the sky, squinting in the sunlight filtering down from the bleachers above us. "It's after twelve."

"Did you just tell the time by looking at the sky?"

He smiles, but it's not enough to show his dimple. He's more tense than I realized, though he wasn't before I started talking. I must have said something that made him nervous. "It's not that hard. Especially in the summer."

"Uh, I'm pretty sure no one else in this century can do that, Jake."

He winces. "You probably shouldn't use my name. I shouldn't have told you in the first place. I shouldn't have let you get into this mess to begin with, and I shouldn't have agreed to the idiotic plan the feds set up, and—"

"Hey!" I squeeze his hand back, scowling at him. "If you start rambling about things you should have done instead of focusing on what you can do now, we're going to get nowhere. I have plenty of time before my meeting, and I want to help you if I can. Just like you're helping me."

He groans, tucking the bloody wipe into the bag and grabbing a fresh one. "I'm not sure anyone can help me at this point."

"What if you tell me as much as you know?"

"You know basically everything already. I was assisting in a setup, something went wrong, and I had to run away to avoid being shot. That's about all I know."

"You're sure he was trying to shoot you?"

"He did shoot. Missed, obviously, but I don't know if he's dirty or if someone tried to set me up." He growls a little, digging a bit too hard into my wound.

I yelp and grab his other hand.

Cringing, he hunches in on himself as if that might make him less dangerous. "I'm sorry. I shouldn't be doing something this important when I'm this riled up. I feel like I haven't taken a breath since this morning." He tries, but it's like he can barely find the strength to inhale. I don't think the sounds of the game and the crowd are helping him, though I've barely noticed it all around us. I've been so focused on him.

Since I'm still holding on to both his hands, I pull him closer and tuck our clasped hands under my chin, resting my head on his fingers. He watches me with so much concern in his green eyes. I can't decide if his concern is more for me or for himself, but it's completely endearing.

"Breathe with me," I tell him.

He pulls his eyebrows together. "You don't have to—"

"*Breathe*, Percival."

He blinks. "Percival?"

"If I can't use your real name, I have to use something, don't I?"

"And you picked *Percival*?"

I nod, taking a deep breath as I do so. "It's a very distinguished name, don't you think?"

"Sure, but I don't think I'm much of a Percival. And I've never been distinguished."

"Okay, then what do you want to be called?"

He shakes his head. "I like when you call me Jake. No one ever uses my real name."

"Really?"

He nods. Swallows. Looks at our hands beneath my chin. "I've spent a long time trying to get away from my name and become someone different from the kid who really was a cyber terrorist."

My heart kicks up a notch, but I ignore it. "So that news article was true?"

"More or less. I never hurt anyone, but I had warped ideas of what the world should be like. Got involved with the wrong people. I thought I was making a difference, but it turns out I was one of the bad guys. I've been trying to make up for it ever since."

He says it all so easily, like being a federally known criminal is no big deal. Yeah, all of his crimes were digital—I'm assuming—but he was probably pretty dangerous if they're using terms like 'cyber terrorism' in relation to him.

"What exactly did you do?" I ask.

He wrinkles his nose, pulling his hands free and returning to my leg. "Would it change your opinion of me if you knew?"

"Probably not."

"Then I'd like to keep the sordid details to myself. I was bad, now I'm good, and that's all you really need to know."

It isn't. I want to know everything about this man, even though I shouldn't.

"Hey, Jake?"

"Hmm?"

"Thanks. For trusting me back."

That catches him off guard, and his mouth hangs open a little as he gapes at me. It's like he didn't think that there was just as much trust on his side as on mine.

I don't know what to say to the look on his face, so I start rambling. "I mean, because I could have totally turned you in to the police or called the FBI even though I don't actually know how to call the FBI. But you let me drive you to wherever I picked and trusted me when I said we should come here even though there are a ton of people around us."

As if on cue, the crowd cheers as one team—the Scorpions, according to the shouts—gets a home run and three players make it back to home plate. They're adorable, and I watch the attractive, blond-haired coach give each boy a high five as they return to their bench. The way he interacts with the kids makes him more attractive, though he's nothing compared to Jake.

"I just think it's cool that we've kind of helped each other so far, you know?" I add with a shrug, and then I turn to look at him.

And while his expression, which falls somewhere between admiration and amusement, is enough to spark something in my chest, it's the way he's touching me that suddenly catches my breath. Not only are his hands as gentle as they've been since the beginning, but his fingers are practically caressing the end of my amputated leg. No one but doctors and my mother have ever touched that part of me. Having someone—more especially an attractive man—touch me without any sign of disgust or discomfort is doing something funny to my insides. It's like there's a hive of bees trapped in there. Nice bees. Bumblebees. The kind you can't help but try to pet because they're so fuzzy and soft-looking.

Jake seems to sense the shift coming over me. His eyebrows pull low as his hold on my leg tightens, and he looks down at the place he touches. "Sorry," he says, pulling away.

I grab his hands and tug them back to where they were. "Don't stop," I beg in a whisper. I've wanted a lot of things in my life, but based on the way I'm currently feeling like a shaken-up soda can about to blow, I've never wanted anything more than a man to accept this part of me.

Color splotches his face as his left hand moves to my other leg, fingers tucking beneath my knee and sending a shiver through me. He swallows, probably realizing that caressing my thighs in any other circumstance would be seen as rather intimate.

Okay, in this circumstance too. The bees inside me are thoroughly enjoying his touch and telling me I should scoot forward until I'm in his lap and close enough that a kiss wouldn't be out of the realm of possibility. I don't know him, he doesn't know me, but there is definitely something humming between us, electric and tangible.

"Isla," he says, and it almost sounds like a warning. Like he knows exactly what's going through my head. But his eyes drop to my mouth anyway, and I know he's considering the idea like I am. I know because his fingers are tightening on my leg as he leans closer.

My phone buzzes between us, alarmingly loud in the dirt.

I groan at the same time Jake sighs, but when I look down to see the message, my heart rate kicks up a notch. It's from Emily Matisse, the woman I'm meeting for lunch. I can only see the first part of the message before my screen goes dark, but the "Hey, something came up" feels ominous.

Jake picks up my phone and holds it toward me when I don't move. "This feels important," he explains when I send him a questioning look.

Though I take my phone—he's right—I tilt my head at him, trying to make sense of this man. "Did you just read my thoughts? Are you psychic?"

His lips twist up in a crooked smile. "No. But I am good with body language, and you are..." He coughs, turning red again. "You're more fluent than most."

Blushing right along with him, I unlock my phone and open the message.

Emily: Hey, something came up. Do you know @biffthe-buffboy? He found out about my meeting with you and insisted on joining us because he's here in Sun City, like me.

I blink, staring at the words but not understanding them. Of course I know Biff. He's like the Ryan Reynolds of the fitness world, with a bazillion followers and every ad endorsement deal in the country. Even people who don't care about fitness know who he is because he reps basically any protein bars that exist. I'm pretty sure he'll be the next Dwayne "The Rock" Johnson because there's a rumor that he's going to be in a movie soon. Basically, he's a big deal.

Jake clears his throat. "Everything okay?"

I don't answer, typing out a response with shaking fingers.

Me: Wait, you're saying Biff is coming to lunch with us?
Emily: I hope that's okay. He said he's seen your work and is interested in collaborating with us, and I couldn't tell him no because his influence alone could be huge for this collab. He could help both of us.
Me: Of course it's okay!
Emily: Did you bring your husband with you to Sun City?

Uh, what? I most definitely don't have a husband. I glance at Jake, in case he really can read minds, but he's still stuck on his worried expression. Why would Emily think I have a husband? I've never posted any pictures except with Cam, and I know I've made it clear that he's my brother-in-law because he's his own level of famous. I didn't want to ruin the popularity he and my sister have, since their whole early relationship was broadcasted for the internet to see. So why would Emily think...?

I swear under my breath and pull up my profile, scrolling to my older posts from a year ago. Last spring I was obsessed with Cam's best friend, Kit, and fancied myself in love with him. There's a high chance I jokingly referred to him as my husband a time or two, and if Emily did her research...

Sure enough, I find a few different posts where I say something about my husband in the caption.

Squirming, I reply to Emily and hope this isn't going to be a big deal.

Me: Why?

The little message that says she's typing pops up. Disappears. Pops up again. It keeps going back and forth for so long that I'm convinced there's a glitch on my phone, but then finally her message appears.

Emily: Biff is a huge flirt. I think he's harmless, but he didn't take me seriously and talk business until he found out I was married and he met Rhys. I think it would be a good idea to bring your husband to lunch with us if you weren't already planning on it. Otherwise, Biff might waste our time because you're too gorgeous for him not to drool all over you. This is my only chance to really talk with you before Rhys and I head to Africa for our humanitarian trip, and I think we need to move quickly if we're going to get any traction together.

Well, that is going to be a problem.

"May I?" Jake says, holding out his hand near my phone. I don't think he's seen any of the messages, but he's clearly seen my frustration and worry in my body language. Or in my head, considering I don't fully believe him when he says he doesn't read minds.

I hesitate but give him my phone, hoping he's smarter than me. I have no idea how to fix this problem.

He reads quickly, one eyebrow rising high. "*Do* you have a husband?"

I wish he were asking under different circumstances. "No." I don't miss the way his shoulders drop in relief, something that does nothing to calm the bees. "But I may have given her reason to think I do."

He hums, still frowning at my phone. "What if you change the meeting place and do it without him?"

I groan. "Because Emily and I both told people where they could meet us if they want to say hi. I can't disappoint any followers who might show up. And if Biff the Buff Boy wants to meet with me, I can't say no to that kind of opportunity."

He clicks on something and starts tapping, though I have no idea what he's doing. "He sounds like he belongs in an eighties movie," he says after a moment.

I snort. "He even looks like the bad guy in *Back to the Future*. I have no idea if Biff is his real name or if he just stole it from those movies."

"It's his real name." Jake frowns at my phone. "And he has a criminal record. Nothing major, but I'd be wary, if I were you."

"First of all, how do you know that? Second, if I was worried about criminal records, I wouldn't be sitting here with you."

He smirks at me, bringing his dimple out in full force. "Fair point. And as for how I know..." He hands my phone back, which is on my Instagram chats again. "It's better if you don't know."

My jaw drops. "Did you just hack into state records or something?"

"Plausible deniability."

"But you used my phone!"

He laughs. "You'll be fine. It was public record, just buried a bit. And no one is looking for *you*."

He had better be right. I'm right on the cusp of making something truly great with my business, and I don't exactly need the FBI hunting me down because I chose to aid a supposed criminal. What will they do to Jake if they catch him? I'm not sure I want to know, mostly because that depends entirely on if he's innocent.

Jake's head tilts to one side again, his expression growing wary. Seriously, either I'm not as skilled at schooling my features as I thought I was, or he is way more than good at reading body lan-

KISS ME IF YOU CAN

guage. "I know I've already said it, but I'm going to keep saying it. You don't have to help me, Isla."

"I might need *you* to help *me*."

That catches him by surprise, his eyebrows shooting high as his mouth drops open ever so slightly. He looks at the baseball diamond, where the Scorpions are now on the field, looks at his hands where they're against the skin of my torn-up legs again, then looks down at my phone. I can practically see the calculations his brain is making as he processes what I just said. He's like that meme incarnate of the blonde woman with the math equations, only he doesn't look as clueless.

In fact, I'm pretty sure he's solved the puzzle. When his eyes rise back up to meet mine, he pulls his eyebrows down, shock turning into disgust. "That's a terrible idea."

I gasp. "Okay, now I'm especially convinced you're psychic."

"Why does everyone always assume... I'm not going to be your husband for your fancy business lunch." He grabs a bandage from the bag and tears the paper open, somehow still gentle despite his agitation as he presses the bandage to my shin, over the worst of my cuts.

I fold my arms. "Why not? You don't even have to say anything. Just exist. Show off your pretty face."

He groans, though the red that rises says something other than frustration. I didn't think a guy like him could get embarrassed. "Isla, you do remember that my face is all over the news right now, right?"

Okay, I might have forgotten that part. Honestly, considering he's literally on the run from the government, the day has been pretty chill so far. "It's not like anyone pays attention to the news."

"You did."

"Only because my brother-in-law mentioned something. *And* because I already knew you were in trouble. You could hide in plain sight!"

He doesn't say anything until he's plastered another few bandages against my skin, gritting his teeth the whole time. "I want to help you," he says when he's satisfied I am properly patched up. "But it's dangerous. I still don't know if it's only the FBI trying to find me, and there is no way I'm putting your life at risk. You're too precious."

His words are already on a swoony level the likes I've never seen, but I can't help but imagine him saying all of this while caressing my cheek with his palm or pressing his forehead against mine. Apparently I've crossed into creepy fantasy-land because he's not even touching me right now.

But I'm pretty sure he wants to. I may not be a mind reader, but I can read body language too. He's tense, but I don't think it's because he's on the run. He wants me, but he doesn't want to want me.

I chew on my lip, noting the way his eyes grow darker as he watches the tiny movement. "You really think I'm precious?" It had better not be in an 'oh, you're so precious, bless your heart' kind of way. I get plenty of that as it is.

Jake swallows and turns his attention to the crowd as they cheer again. "I think you've been underestimated too much in your life."

My heart pounds in a steady rhythm in my chest, loud enough that I'm sure he hears it. "What do you mean?"

He closes his eyes, looking pained. "I mean you are the strongest, bravest, most beautiful woman I've ever met, and I hate that people aren't smart enough to look past your physical difference and see the remarkable person who doesn't let it hold her back."

Tears fill my eyes, even though I can't stop thinking about how there is no crying in baseball, according to Tom Hanks. I need to reply to Emily's last message, and I need to convince Jake that it's a good idea to come with me and help me get this collaboration going. But right now, I need to find a way to thank this man for being kind.

I leap onto him so quickly that I expect to either knock him over or for him to turn into a stone statue. Neither happens. Jake must have been ready for me because his arms wrap around me in a tight hold. He's not a big guy by any means, but there's something about his embrace that *feels* big, like he's the kind of guy who can protect me from all the hurts on the inside as well as the outside.

"You don't have to come with me," I say into his shoulder. "You're right, and it would only put you at risk."

"That isn't what I said." His arms tug me tighter against his body, and I can feel his resolve slipping the longer he holds me. "It's you I'm worried about, Isla. But..."

I hold my breath.

"But I owe you. After everything you've done for me this morning, I..." He grimaces. "Okay. I'll be your husband."

I barely hold back a squeal of delight.

Chapter Five

Jake

I'm just full of bad decisions today. Starting with agreeing to help the FBI—worst decision of the year—today has consistently gone downhill, and I'm honestly surprised I haven't hit the bottom yet. One minute I think things are as bad as they could be, and the next I'm agreeing to be a virtual stranger's fake husband instead of lying low.

Now I'm walking into a public library where I'm bound to be recognized or caught as soon as I sit down at one of the computers because Isla insisted I try to get some answers while we still have time.

"Would you relax?" Isla hisses to me. She's smiling brightly beside me, like she doesn't have a care in the world. "You look anxious, and that's going to make people nervous."

"It may come as a shock, but I *am* anxious." I wish we had stopped at a thrift store *before* coming to the library; people keep eyeing my bright blue pants and giving me judging looks. My outfit is probably getting me more attention than my torn-up suit would have.

Isla nods to one of the librarians, who averts her eyes as soon as she sees Isla's missing leg. "*I* know you're anxious, but you don't want anyone else to know! Take a deep breath, Jake."

She said that same thing under the bleachers, and it did help. But we were basically alone then, despite the crowd above us, and we're definitely not alone now.

Even if I would like to be.

"Hey." Isla stops, grabbing my arm to stop me along with her. Then she reaches up and places her palm against my cheek.

Instinctively, I grab her elbow to keep her steady even though I'm pretty sure she has excellent balance. I probably just want to be closer to her because her blue eyes seem to pierce my soul, especially when we're close like this. She sees so much when I wish she wouldn't.

"I'm sorry," I say.

She smiles. "I didn't say anything."

"You were going to tell me I'm going to ruin your lunch meeting if I can't get a grip."

Though I wish we weren't standing in the middle of the library, I can't move because she's leaning on me now. She knows this, which makes her smile grow. "Jake, you can't control everything in life, and I wasn't going to say anything about the lunch. Right now, we're here for you. And you need to breathe."

I shake my head. "We're wasting time. I don't need—"

"You need to figure out what happened at the park, and we have plenty of time." Her thumb brushes across my cheek in a tantalizingly soft touch. "Take a breath with me, Jake."

I do, even while my eyes dart around the library to make sure no one is giving us attention they shouldn't.

"No, stay focused. Look at me."

I couldn't ignore that order if I wanted to. My eyes slide back to hers, which are fixed on me above a pert nose and a warm smile on her pink lips. Everything about this woman is beautiful, and I'm not talking about her physical features. No one has ever taken the time to see me like this, and they certainly haven't spent any energy helping me. I've always been on my own, looking out for myself, making my own choices and dealing with the consequences.

Isla has every reason to hate me and leave me behind, but she's here, calming me down so I can try to save my own life.

"Breathe," she whispers.

I lean in close and take a breath when she does.

"One more time."

"You've clearly done this before," I murmur. It's not a complaint, but concern colors my words.

Isla shrugs. "My mom gets panic attacks all the time. So does my brother-in-law. And everyone struggles with anxiety now and then, so it's not like this is some breakthrough in calming someone down."

The first time the FBI caught me, I was in my apartment downtown. I tried to run, and I got so panicked that I only made it a block or two before I couldn't breathe anymore. The man who cuffed me and took me in didn't even have to chase me down. Outside of fighting against firewalls and viruses, which isn't as exciting as it is in the movies, I've lived relatively stress-free since getting let out on parole. This whole anxiety thing is relatively new to me.

I don't like it.

"I feel like I'm wearing a hundred pounds of wool coats," I admit, holding her elbow a little tighter.

Isla's expression softens. "That's normal in high-stress situations. That's why breathing is so important. The more you breathe, the lighter you'll feel."

I believe her, but that doesn't change the situation. "We're wasting time. I can breathe at a computer."

Though she sighs, she nods. "I'll concede, but only because I want you to have as much time as you need. We need to find a computer that's still logged in because we don't have a library card to use."

She resituates her crutches and then leads the way, even though I feel like I should be the one taking charge. This is my problem we're trying to fix, and we're in my city. But I follow her anyway, trying to breathe in deeply like she said. Hopefully, I won't need much time to get some more information, but I have to make sure no one realizes what I'm doing or they might alert someone. The last thing I want is for the feds to come storming into the library.

"If something goes wrong," I mutter, stepping as close to Isla as I can while we walk, "you have to pretend you have nothing to do with me. The FBI can't do anything to you if they don't know you exist."

She pauses, looking back with her eyebrows pulled low. "You want me to just leave you behind?"

"Yes." No. I don't actually want that. I don't know why, but I want to spend as much time with her as I can, and that's a huge problem. Even if I manage to evade the FBI long enough for Isla's meeting to go smoothly, I can't run from them forever. I've gotten lucky so far, and without some way to clear my name and prove my innocence—against what, I still don't know—I'll be a fugitive until I'm caught. Any time I spend with Isla is borrowed time, and I can't afford to get attached.

Isla doesn't respond to my request, instead keeping her focus on the row of computers at the back of the library. "Aha!" she gestures to one that isn't on the login screen, though a little timer at the bottom says I only have fifteen minutes before I'm logged out. "Your sword, Sir Percival."

I slip into the chair and open up the browser. It's going to have all sorts of blockers and filters, which will take time to work around. "I'd call this more of my steed," I mutter, losing myself in the process. I keep a small amount of my focus on the woman next to me, but I'm banking on her paying attention to our surroundings because I only have so much focus to go around. "My intelligence is my sword."

Isla snickers. "Nice and humble, I see."

"I'm good at what I do."

She's quiet for a few minutes, giving me a chance to start digging into surveillance footage of the street just beyond the park. There weren't any cameras at that particular park, which is why Hadley chose it, but maybe I can find something beyond it. I'll only hack into the FBI's feed as a last resort because I won't be able to hide my location if I get inside. They'll be on me in minutes.

"Do you know what this reminds me of?" Isla asks after a while. She's spinning back and forth in her chair like she's bored.

I grunt.

"It's like that scene in Captain America, you know? Where he and Black Widow are at the mall and trying to locate the bad guy."

"I never saw that movie."

"Boo. It's so good!"

I flash a quick smile. "I haven't seen a lot of movies lately. I've been too busy trying to protect the world against people like me."

"What's funny about the scene is one of the employees comes up to them, and they have to cover what they're trying to do. Natasha says they're looking for a honeymoon destination, and the guy totally buys it even though there's no way he wouldn't recognize Captain America."

"Uh huh."

"Wouldn't it be funny if we had to do something like that? Of course, I would be Captain America in this scenario."

She says that right as I pull up a satellite video of the park in the hopes of getting a sense of where everything was happening and what might be happening now. Though there's not much activity in the park right now, I'm glad I pulled this up. My bench is there in plain view, but there's a large bunch of shrubs right behind where I was sitting that I didn't notice. The street is right behind those shrubs, but it's not the street where the FBI van was. They were on the other side of the park. That feels like a serious oversight on the FBI's part, when pretty much anyone could sneak up on me. Did they do that on purpose to make it easier to take me out?

But it was Fields who pointed his gun at me. In plain sight. The FBI aren't known for flashing their guns unless they absolutely have to.

What if he wasn't pointing at me after all?

"Do you two need help finding anything?"

I jump at the sound of a soft, feminine voice, heart stuttering in my chest and my breath catching in my lungs.

A middle-aged librarian glances between us before locking her eyes on my computer screen. It's not necessarily odd to look at a satellite image, but because this is most definitely a live video, she seems to be putting pieces together as she looks at the other tabs I have pulled open. And when she looks back at me, recognition sparks to life in her eyes.

Suddenly, Isla throws her arms around me from behind and tucks her chin over my shoulder. "We're trying to find a venue for our wedding!" she says loudly.

The librarian shushes her and takes a step back. "That's a lovely park," she says, her voice hushed to demonstrate proper library etiquette. "When is the big day?"

"End of November." Still too loud, Isla presses a kiss to my cheek that leaves a burning spot behind. "I just about died when I saw that fountain. Can't you imagine a bunch of lights strung around the place and the water splashing as a backdrop to the ceremony?"

I don't know if she's asking me or the librarian, but I have nothing to say regardless. I'm still trying to catch my breath again. Weirdly, I *can* imagine it, though. And I can see Isla in a stunning lace dress that highlights her slender frame and leaves my mouth feeling dry.

"My Percy told me I could have whatever I wanted. Isn't he just the sweetest?" She kisses me again, pressing her hands against my chest in a far too familiar way for someone I met only a couple of hours ago.

Meeting the librarian's eyes, I force a smile. "I'm just glad she said yes," I choke out because my mouth has literally gone dry.

With one more glance at the computer, the librarian nods and then gives Isla a smile. "You only have a few minutes left, so if you need more time, I can help you up at the front desk."

"Thank you!" Isla says brightly. Still too loud. And even though the librarian wanders away, she doesn't move her arms from where they're pressed against me. "I can't believe that worked!"

I groan and click out of all of the windows I had open. I didn't get any actual answers, but I don't have time to do any more digging. We need to get new clothes for Isla's meeting anyway. "Thank you," I tell her, putting my hand over her arm and holding her in place. I don't want her to let go, which feels like a problem. "You're a genius."

"Or I watch too many movies." To my surprise, she presses one more kiss to my cheek before gathering up her crutches. There's no one to pretend for, and the feel of her lips leaves me momentarily stunned. "Come on, sweetie pie, I saw a thrift store just down the road."

Chapter Six
Jake

THIS ISN'T HOW THINGS are supposed to happen. I'm no expert in matters of the heart, but I do know it takes more than a couple of hours to fall for someone. There needs to be familiarity, common interests, similar goals. A couple needs to know each other's flaws as well as the good traits. Know what they fear and what they most want in life. Love comes from time and growth and experience.

So why do I feel like I'm falling for Isla Adams?

As she peruses a thrift store downtown, I can't take my eyes off of her, even though I'm pretending to browse the records so I don't look shifty. She navigates the store with ease on her crutches, which doesn't surprise me, but I *am* surprised that she hasn't once complained about missing her prosthesis. I'm sure she prefers having free use of her hands, but she's over there smiling like she's having the best day of her life.

I've never met anyone like her. From the moment I literally ran into her, she's been calm and kind and genuinely interested in my fate, despite every reason to hate and distrust me. Maybe that's why I'm so drawn to her.

She's the first person in years—maybe ever—to truly see me. To give me any sort of attention and respect without me demanding it with a demonstration of my skills or talents. My team respects me, and they all seem to like working for me, but most of them joined my company because they'd heard of me from my darker days and were more curious than anything. But Isla?

Isla hasn't given any heed to my background or my job. She only seems to care about *me*.

A woman approaches her, ducking in close to speak to her, and then points over at me.

I stiffen, preparing to run, but Isla shakes her head and says something back with a smile and a laugh. Though the woman lingers, looking skeptical as she takes me in, she eventually wanders off, and Isla comes over to my section of the store with a bunch of stuff slung over her shoulder.

"She warned me that some guy was staring at me," she says as she reaches me. "I told her that it was just my dorky husband. These are for you."

I take the clothes from her shoulder and grimace. It looks like most of a three-piece suit. "I don't really wear suits," I mumble, though the words come out softer than my usual dislike would warrant. I think I like the sound of being Isla's husband more than I should, given the circumstances.

Isla shrugs. "Yeah, well, my husband wouldn't be wandering around in women's sweatpants, considering my profession. Get changed while I find myself something to wear."

I want to argue. I really do. If I'm going to pull off a fake marriage, even for just a few hours, I'm going to need to be able to relax. And I've never been relaxed in a suit. Outside of graduation, the only other times I've worn suits have been for my parents' funerals, so it's not like this outfit is going to conjure good memories. I wore the suit at graduation because my foster mom insisted on it, and I needed to keep her moderately happy so she wouldn't wonder what I was doing during all that time I spent on the computer.

"Please, Jake," Isla says. There's a bit of fear in her eyes for the first time all day, which means this business lunch is a bigger deal than I realized. I may spend all day on the internet, but it's not the same way she does it. I'm going to assume most of her marketing is through social media and word of mouth. How can I refuse her when she's already done so much to help me? Without her, I never would have made it out of the park.

Holding back a groan, I spin on my heel and head for the dressing rooms. I still think going to lunch with her is a bad idea, but she might be on to something with hiding in plain sight. It worked at the library, and so far no one has stopped to look too closely at my face since we've come into the store. It doesn't solve my problem, but hiding with her is buying me time. Time that I, so far, haven't used to figure out a plan.

I've been too busy falling for Isla.

By the time I've wrangled myself into the suit, which fits surprisingly well considering it's secondhand, Isla is waiting for me outside the dressing room in a blue floral dress that hugs her body in a way that makes my mouth go dry again. Outside of the scrapes and cuts on her arms and legs, she looks fresh and fabulous, like she is more than ready to tackle the rest of this day. From her fair skin to her long, blonde hair, to the crystal-blue eyes she appraises me with, she's the most beautiful woman I've ever seen. And that says nothing about her strength, intelligence, or kindness, all of which she has in ample supply.

I might be in trouble. We're not going to mention how close I came to kissing her at the park. Even before the ruse at the library, kissing her was all I could think about. And I am not and never have been a guy who kisses on a first date, let alone within the first few hours of knowing someone, so I'm pretty sure Isla has put me under some kind of spell.

Not that I believe in magic. But if anyone can make me believe in something like that, she could. It's the only explanation for why I keep imagining our wedding day at the park even though none of this is real.

"So?" Isla says, setting aside her crutches and balancing on her foot as she holds out her hand to me.

I take hold of her fingers and let her tug me closer to her. "So, what?"

"This suit can't be that bad, can it? You're wearing it so well." She buttons my cuff for me because I couldn't get it one-handed.

I generally avoid buttons because buttons mean fancy. I don't do fancy.

I put on a smile and gently place a hand on her waist to help her balance as she buttons my other cuff. "The only reason I'm wearing this is because you asked me to," I tell her.

Her cheeks blossom with pink as she moves to tie my loose tie, which happens to match her dress rather well. "You sure you want to help me?"

I'm sure I don't have a choice. "I want to do whatever I can to make this work for you." I honestly haven't dated much over the years, which is becoming increasingly obvious the longer I'm around this woman. In high school, I was the depressed kid who lost both his parents within a year. Then I was a cyber terrorist with a vendetta against anyone and anything under the guise of making the world a better place. As soon as I turned myself around, I poured my heart into my work and haven't stopped since.

Isla's hopeful smile makes me want to drop everything to make her happy, and I've never felt that way. Sure, I help thousands of people every year as I track down cyber criminals and put a stop to their illegal activities, but I've never focused on someone beyond the bounds of a screen. She may have been spitting lies when she told the librarian that I would give her anything she wanted, but it's starting to feel true.

Isla finishes with my tie, letting her hands rest against my chest. I wrap my arm more securely around her, ignoring the temptation to pull her closer. She'll be going back to Diamond Springs as soon as her meeting is over, and I have to remind myself that I have too many obligations here to follow her. Not to mention the likelihood of me going to prison once I'm caught. Even if this day hadn't started as wild as it did, our relationship—if I can call it that—still wouldn't be able to go anywhere.

"Have you ever been married?" she asks out of the blue.

My chest grows tight beneath her fingers, which are burning me with their heat even through the vest I'm wearing. "No."

"Me neither. Do you think we can pull this off? I mean, it's not like being married is the deciding factor in whether or not I get these collaborations, but Emily's pretty convinced that Biff will only talk business if I'm off the market."

I hate that phrase, *off the market*. It cheapens the value of a person and leaves them worth nothing but their marital status. Isla isn't for sale and never will be, even if a part of me is pretty convinced I would be the first to bid.

I clear my throat before my mind conjures up images of Isla standing in front of a sea of men all hoping to take her home. I'd rather think of her in that fictional wedding dress with eyes only for me.

"I don't think there's much we need to say to convince them," I say with a shrug. I reach up and take her hand as she plays with my tie, tucking my fingers around hers like I've done it a million times. "We just have to act like we like each other. Some marriages don't achieve even that much, so we'll be ahead of the game. Why did Emily think you have a husband in the first place?"

I don't miss the way she turns bright red just before she buries her face into my chest to hide. Her embarrassment is palpable as she sinks into me, her whole body leaning into my hold. I'm more than happy to oblige.

"It's so stupid," she says, slightly muffled, "but last year I had a huge crush on my brother-in-law's best friend, and I was convinced we were going to end up together. I hadn't really started my business yet, so I did a lot of random posts, and I talked about him a lot. I called him my husband because I was so sure he would be."

Something growls to life inside me, like a little gremlin ready to crawl its way free and go scratch up this mystery man's face. Apparently my jealousy monster isn't all that vicious if scratching is the worst it can come up with.

"What happened to your crush?" I ask, even though I shouldn't.

Isla sighs, long and heavy. "He's getting married next month. To a woman so perfect for him that I can't even be mad about it."

"I think you can be a little mad." I know I am. What kind of idiot passes on someone like Isla? "So, Emily thinks you have a husband, and we need Biff to think so as well because he is definitely going to be interested in you."

She scoffs. "I doubt that. He's a huge fitness guy, and I'm..." She gestures to her missing leg like that explains what she is. Then she giggles. "My sister and her husband are both health junkies, and they've tried so hard to get me to work out and put a little muscle on these twigs of mine." She wiggles her arms even though I'm still holding onto one of her hands. "But I am way more interested in my sewing machine and a pair of scissors than I am in kettlebells and burpees."

"I don't even know what those are," I admit before I can stop myself.

Her little laugh into my chest makes the slight humiliation worth it. But then she speaks. "You are so different from the man I would have picked for myself, Jake."

Oh. Yeah, that makes sense, and I really shouldn't be disappointed because we're not in a relationship to begin with. But I am disappointed, and my mind is scrambling to come up with ways to get me closer to what she might have imagined for herself. I can start going to the gym and lifting weights. Maybe get a phone. Start wearing more suits?

A shudder runs through me. I like Isla, but I'm not sure I like her *that* much. Besides, I'm more likely to end up in federal prison before the day is out than for Isla to decide she actually wants to be with me.

Clearing my throat, I reach for her crutches leaning against the wall and hold them ready for her. "We need to find some wedding rings," I tell her, which doesn't help diminish my fantasies of this somehow becoming real.

"Oh." She looks at her left hand, which is still pressed up against my chest. "I didn't even think about that!"

"There was a pawn shop a couple of doors down from here. I'm sure we can find something there." Though, I wish I had waited to say anything because I like holding her a little too much. As soon as she pulls away and situates herself with her crutches, my fingers are missing the warmth of her body. The fabric of her dress is thin enough that I could feel each curve of her skin as I held her, and my body aches to get her back.

Isla nods and starts leading the way to the checkout, which will get interesting because we're already wearing everything we're purchasing. "Good idea. Let's hope they have something big and gaudy to really make Biff believe I'm taken." She pauses, looking back at me. "And fake. No point in spending lots of money on a fake marriage, right?"

"Right," I agree automatically. Then I realize what she said. It makes sense logically, but I really don't like the idea of her wearing something not worthy of being on her finger.

Clearly I'm coming unhinged if I'm thinking about crossing the street to check out the jewelry store while Isla goes to the pawn shop.

Thankfully, the clerk at checkout doesn't bat an eye as we hand him the tags from our new outfits, though his gaze does linger a little too long on Isla's missing leg.

Instinct pulls me closer to her, and I wrap my arm around her waist and tuck my chin over her shoulder. Though she shivers beneath my touch, she leans into me and relaxes.

The clerk turns his full focus to our purchases.

"Already feeling possessive?" Isla mutters to me.

"You have no idea." She smells incredible, which is impressive given what she's been through today. I have to resist the urge to inhale deeply. "What kind of husband would I be if I didn't protect you?"

"You know I don't need your protection, right?"

I chuckle. "Does that mean you don't want it?"

"Of course not."

The clerk gives us our total, and before Isla can tap her phone to the reader, I slide a hundred-dollar bill across the counter.

Isla groans. "What? No! This is my business lunch, so I'm paying for it."

"Too late," I argue, since the clerk is already putting it into his till. Plus, the more we can avoid anyone tracking us with credit cards, the safer we'll be. I'm still not sure if anyone has connected me to Isla, but I won't take any chances.

Isla takes my change and stuffs it into my hand where it rests around her middle. "You are incredibly frustrating, husband."

"No doubt one of my many flaws."

I don't fully hear what she mumbles back, but it sounds a lot like, "Or the only one."

I've never really been one to need an ego boost, but I'm not mad about getting this one. I'm pretty sure I have a dorky grin on my face as we head out into the heat and make our way to the pawn shop.

As I pull the door open for Isla, she nudges me lightly. "Don't get a big head, cyber man. I could never marry an egomaniac."

I put a hand over my heart. "I am a picture of humility." Usually, that's true. I know I've done bad stuff in the past, and while I'm smart, there's a lot about life I don't understand. Especially socially, Isla is far better off than I am despite being a few years younger than me. I don't know exactly how old she is, though I've been tempted to borrow her phone again and find out more about her. There are probably better ways.

"What's your favorite color?" I ask her as we step inside the shop.

We're hit with a wave of air conditioning and an assortment of bad smells, from cigarette smoke to must to a general human body smell that makes my stomach churn. I'd hoped this would be less like the stereotypical pawn shop and more like a classy little store with the perfect set of rings waiting for us on a velvet pillow.

What can I say? I am an optimist. Ha! I wasn't before Isla.

Isla raises an eyebrow as she moves to one of the glass cases along the wall. "It depends on the day."

"What's your favorite color today?"

"Green." She glances at me and turns pink.

Hmm. My eyes are green. "I like blue," I tell her, which deepens her blush. "Favorite food?"

She crouches down, using her crutches for balance as she examines the jewelry lower in the case. I should probably help her look, but I'm too busy watching her. "Suddenly curious about your wife?"

I can't stop the smile that pulls at my lips at the sound of her calling herself my wife. I'm regretting this plan less and less. "Of course. The more I know about you, the more I can keep the Buff Boy away from you."

"How is my favorite food going to keep him away from me? It's French fries, by the way, but I rarely get to eat them."

"Why?"

"Because I have to avoid salty foods so my prosthesis will fit right, and unsalted fries are the worst."

I wouldn't have even thought about how much diet could affect the way her prosthesis fits. I'm suddenly aware of my body and how functional all of my limbs are.

Isla laughs when she looks at me. "It's fine, Jake. I've lived this way for a decade and a half. If I really want to eat fries, I just have to prepare to go legless the next day. But most of the time my diet is pretty healthy. What's your favorite food?"

Anything I can make in ten minutes or less. I eat out more than I should, and half the time I don't care what I'm eating. It's just a way to keep me going. "Depends on the day," I say, using her own answer. "Did you always want to design clothes?"

She smirks. "I wanted to be a ballerina."

I really hope she's joking. But even if she's not, she doesn't seem too beat up by the idea that ballet would be a lot more difficult with one biological leg instead of two. She would have made a great ballerina, whether on two legs or one.

"Did you always want to work with computers?"

"Yeah." I sound boring by comparison. "Just maybe not along the path I took."

"Maybe?" She winks at me before moving on to the next glass case.

An employee finally appears from the back room, looking us over with narrowed eyes. I should probably help Isla with the search, so I approach him with an easy smile.

"What do you have for wedding rings?" I ask, seriously hoping Isla's theory about hiding in plain sight is correct. I'm shooting for the most casual posture I can manage, though I don't know if "casual" can be achieved if you have to try.

The man, who looks far too normal for someone who works in a pawn shop, grunts and pulls out a box from underneath the counter in between us. It holds an assortment of jeweled rings and simple bands, so I pretty much just need to find the right sizes.

Before I can even reach for the first ring that looks like a possibility, Isla shrieks.

I jump and spin, expecting to find Frank Hadley with a knife to her throat, but Isla is still alone, pointing to something in the case in front of her.

"That's my leg!" she says.

I press a hand over my heart, trying to calm it down. I'm not sure a man can survive this much stress in a day. "What?"

"My leg! He has my leg!"

I hurry over to her. "Are you sure?" I ask, though that's a stupid question. It still has her shoe attached to it, the opposite to the one on her foot. The poor prosthesis looks a little battered, but hopefully it didn't sustain too much damage. "Where did you get this?" I ask the employee. According to his nametag, his name is Geoff. Geoff with a G, a spelling I've always hated for some reason.

Geoff shrugs, folding his arms. "Bought it."

That's generally how pawn shops work, but it's only been a couple of hours since the park. Who would have found it and brought it here, of all places? I highly doubt many people wander down that ravine.

"It's mine," Isla tells Geoff, her voice wobbling a bit. She's been incredibly calm about her missing prosthesis, but I'm sure she wants it back. She probably thought, like me, that it would be waiting for her at the park as soon as it was safer to go look for it. "I need it back."

Geoff grunts. "You can't prove that it's yours."

Isla gestures to the missing bottom half of her left leg.

"That doesn't mean anything. Plenty of people are missing legs."

"It has my shoe on it!"

"That's a pretty common shoe."

It isn't. It's not name brand, and the teal and lime green colors are uncommon for footwear. Geoff is clearly hoping to turn a profit on this leg, and I worry Isla's desperation isn't going to make it cheap.

"How much?" I ask, keeping my voice calm and cool.

Geoff narrows his eyes at me. "Well now, that's a good question, isn't it? Legs like that are expensive."

I don't even want to know how much a prosthesis like hers costs. Because her leg was amputated above the knee, it takes a lot more for her to get a functional device that works for her. She has one of the nice ones too, the kind that has a computer chip and motorized functions.

I fold my arms to match our new friend. "Whatever you paid for it, we'll pay you more. How much for the leg, Geoff?"

With a greedy gleam in his eyes, he smiles. "Ten grand."

Those two words feel like a punch to the gut. "You can't be serious."

Isla groans. "That's more than what I paid for it with my insurance," she mutters so only I can hear. "But it's worth more than that."

I put my hand on the small of her back, feeling her tension and frustration in her stiff muscles. "I'll give you a thousand," I tell Geoff, hoping to call his bluff and that he doesn't actually know the value of a prosthesis like that.

Geoff laughs. "No way."

"No one else can even use it," Isla argues. "It was made specifically for me, so you're not going to get any money for it. I'll give you two thousand."

Geoff shakes his head.

As I try to think of some way to convince him to give us the leg, my thoughts stray in a direction I wish they wouldn't. I could so easily hack into the store's finances and steal the money back after I pay for the leg. They might not even notice it missing if I do it right. I swore to myself years ago that I would never go down that path again, but it would be for a good cause. Isla needs her leg back, and there's no way I'm letting her spend ten thousand dollars when it's my fault she lost it in the first place.

But Isla sighs, shaking her head as she hobbles forward. I'm about to stop her from making a mistake when she starts perusing the box of rings, looking like her world just collapsed in on her.

Yeah, stealing from the shop sounds like a great idea.

I want to tell Isla not to waste her time or give the man any of our money, but we do need rings, and we're running out of time. Her meeting is in less than twenty minutes. With a sigh to match hers, I join her at the counter and find the most basic silver ring, slipping it onto my finger and praising the fact that it fits.

I don't bother asking Geoff how much the ring costs. I doubt it's worth much, so I slap a hundred on the counter and give him a glare that says he had better not argue. He doesn't.

Isla takes a little longer, but she eventually finds a simple fake diamond on a rose gold band. It's not what I would have expected from her, but she smiles as she slips it on and holds it out to admire it.

When I try to hand over another bill, Isla grabs my wrist and shakes her head. "Not this time," she says sharply. Either she's annoyed that I keep paying for things, or she's still upset about the prosthesis chilling in a case on the other side of the room. Maybe it's both. I cringe as she taps her phone to the card reader, but it's probably better if I don't argue. I don't want to put her in a worse mood right before her big meeting.

"Anything else I can do for the two of you?" Geoff asks, grinning at us like he just got ten thousand bucks. I'm pretty sure Isla is right, and unless someone buys the leg for parts, it's not going to be a lot of help for anyone. A person who can afford to spend ten grand on a prosthetic leg isn't going to be looking for one in a pawn shop.

"No," I growl at Geoff, fingers itching to sneak into his system and take a look around. I won't actually do it, but the temptation is still there.

Isla leads the way to the door but pauses halfway there, looking back at me with narrowed eyes.

I squirm. Did she somehow figure out that I'm thinking thoughts I shouldn't? "What?"

"I think I need to do something with your hair," she says.

I really don't like the sound of that, though I resist the urge to cover it with my hands. "What's wrong with my hair?"

"It doesn't match your suit. And Emily will probably expect my husband to be a little more..."

Grimacing, I look down at my scuffed-up shoes that will hopefully go unnoticed. "Fashion-forward?" I supply. That is certainly not a term I would ever use to describe myself, but it would make sense given Isla's profession. "Do you have time to fix my hair?"

She shrugs. "I'll run over to the drugstore next door. Meet you at the car?"

I nod, and as she hurries out the door, I glance at the prosthesis behind me before meeting Geoff's smug gaze.

Chapter Seven

Isla

With a bit of hair gel and some bottled water, I manage to get Jake's hair to look moderately stylish, though he could really use a haircut. I get the sense he doesn't care much about the way he looks, which is weirdly refreshing after years of being in the fashion world. Most guys I interact with are either gym bros, courtesy of my sister and her husband, or snobby designers who tend to look at me with disdain. Not a lot of down-to-earth guys take any interest in someone like me, and I didn't realize how much I craved that until I met Jake.

It's why I liked Kit so much, even if I never looked too hard at my crush on Cam's friend. He was—is—such a chill guy and has always cared more about the people around him than about himself. Jake's the same way, even though I know he hates everything I just did to his hair as he examines himself in my car window.

"I'm washing all of this junk out as soon as this is over," he mutters, grimacing at his reflection. "It looks good, though."

I snicker. "It looks better than good. You're a Hottie McBody, Jake Moody."

He loses the battle against his smile, letting it loose as he looks at me. "Well, are you ready for this?"

"Nope, but I don't have much of a choice. Are *you* ready?"

He shrugs, sticking his hands into his pockets and looking way too delicious in his suit. The suit didn't have a jacket with it, but it's too hot for him to be comfortable in one anyway. With his trim torso, he's wearing the heck out of that vest, and I'm dying a little inside knowing I can't post a picture of the two of us. My followers would eat him up, especially if he flashed that dimple. He's the perfect book boyfriend, neighborhood crush, dream man combination, just as pretty on the inside as he is on the outside.

Maybe after my meeting I can help him clear his name and we can...what? Hang out a few more hours before I head home? It should be weird that I'm already missing a guy I've only known for a few hours, but an ache has settled in my stomach thinking about how this day has to end at some point.

We climb into the car, Jake behind the wheel as if he's done that a million times. I can almost picture us taking road trips together and switching off every few hours so the other person can nap. I don't know what kind of music Jake likes, but he'd probably sing off-key with me to Taylor Swift because he'd know her music makes me happy. We'd share snacks and eat way too much candy and beef jerky, and we would stop at random attractions in the middle of nowhere just to get a weird keychain with a ball of twine on it.

I don't know why my brain went straight to the World's Largest Ball of Twine when we're nowhere near Kansas, but apparently peak romance is weirdness on the road.

I'm blaming the library. I was totally joking when I brought up the Captain America stuff, and then that snooty librarian came over and started looking at Jake too hard. Either I knew she was going to recognize him or I was just feeling jealous of anyone looking at him, but I panicked and went straight for lovey-dovey. I didn't expect to enjoy holding him as much as I did! It took everything in me not to plant a legit kiss on his mouth.

And oh, how I wanted to kiss him. I can only imagine what that would be like when he seems to be so in control of everything. Would he kiss with precision and intention, or would he go the complete opposite of his personality and kiss with abandon? Either way, I know it would be amazing.

"This is it, right?" Jake says, pulling me out of my fantasy.

I blink, staring at the restaurant where I agreed to meet Emily. *Focus, Isla.* La Bella was highly rated online, and it looked fancy enough in the pictures that I could feel semi-professional while doing my best not to completely fangirl over one of my idols. Hopefully Emily agrees with me.

"Yeah, this is it," I breathe.

Jake takes hold of my hand, giving it a squeeze. "You're going to do great, Isla. And I'll be right beside you the whole time, however you need me."

"Is it weird that I'm glad you're here?" I turn to him and bite my lip, forcing myself to ignore *his* lips. I need to be Business Isla now, not Kiss a Stranger Isla. But Jake doesn't feel like a stranger anymore. Honestly, he never did.

I clear my throat. "I mean, I was so ready to conquer this meeting and girl boss so hard, but now that I'm here, I don't think I would be able to get out of the car because I'm so nervous."

"It's hard to imagine you being afraid of anything," he says with an adorable smirk. Dang it, now I'm looking at his mouth. "After all, you weren't afraid of me."

I shove him, laughing along with him. "That's because you're not scary."

I take a deep breath and force myself to be brave. It's not like I haven't done collaborations before, but this is the first time I've ever met with someone in person. Especially someone as famous as Emily Matisse. When it comes to social media, she's everything I want to be. Then there's Biff, who is going to be his own version of Goliath. Hopefully in the sense of his size and influence, not in the sense that tiny little David (me) has to defeat him. I like to think I'm fierce, but I'm not exactly a slayer of giants.

One more deep breath, and then I repeat some affirmations to myself.

I am a strong, confident woman who doesn't back down from a challenge. I am valid in the sphere of my career. I am more than my limitations. I can do anything I set my mind to as long as I don't give up.

Jake squeezes my hand again, giving me a wide smile. "Whatever you just did, you're standing taller. So to speak."

I snort a laugh. "Hard to stand when you're sitting in a car, but I get your meaning. Ready?"

He nods. "If you are."

"I'm terrified. But that's not going to change. Let's go."

I wish I could hold Jake's hand as we walk up to the front door, just to keep up the contact which is surprisingly comforting, but I content myself with his hand on my back instead. Now that we're here, he seems to be breathing easier, like he's already forgotten his own problems and is simply here to help me with mine. I could kiss the guy if I wasn't about to be late for my meeting.

But maybe I have time?

"Isla!" So much for time. Emily waves at us as soon as we step through the door, her smile wide and genuine. And goodness me, she's more gorgeous in person than she is in photos, which I didn't think could be possible. She makes me feel frumpy by comparison, even if I kind of love this dress I found.

The man behind her is easy to recognize as her husband, Rhys, who has made plenty of appearances in her posts. Though he's on the phone, he still smiles my way and proves that men are capable of being courteous even when they have nothing to gain.

"Emily," I breathe, relaxing under her warm gaze. "I can't thank you enough for being willing to meet me."

"Are you kidding?" She pulls me in for a hug, nearly knocking one of my crutches out from under my hand. Jake reaches out to keep me steady, a silent protector just behind me. "I've wanted to meet you for ages!"

A squeak pops out of me. "You have?"

But Emily's eyes have shifted to Jake, and I can already tell her focus is all on him now. "And you must be the mysterious man she keeps hidden away. What's your name, handsome?"

I don't think she's flirting with him. If she is, her husband is being awfully cool about it. But even though I'm pretty sure she's just being friendly, a gremlin growls to life inside me, wanting me to bat Emily's hand away from Jake's.

Jake shakes her hand but lets go quickly, which I appreciate. "I'm Marty," he says. "Isla has been talking about this meeting for months."

My stomach drops at the same time Emily frowns. "We only set this up a couple of weeks ago," she says, glancing between us as if she knows our marriage is a total sham.

Jake, on the other hand, doesn't flinch. "Oh, I know, but this piñata of mine sure knows how to manifest. She's been begging the universe to throw you two together." Then he wraps his arms around me, pulling me flush against his chest. "Isn't that right?"

Rhys says something to Emily, pulling her attention away from us long enough for me to say, "Piñata? What? And where did the name Marty come from?"

Jake chuckles, and the sound reverberates against my ribcage. "The name felt fitting for the situation."

"And the piñata?"

He presses his nose into my neck and sends a shiver through me. "I knew I wanted to hit that the moment I saw you."

I snort a laugh loud enough that I'm lucky a bunch of snot doesn't come flying out of my nose. If Jake wasn't holding on to me, I would probably be on the floor and dying of laughter. "That's the worst joke I've ever heard," I gasp, though I can't say I hate the implication.

When Jake replies, he speaks in a whisper in my ear that makes me shiver. "I thought you would enjoy that one."

"Oh my gosh, you two are adorable," Emily says. She practically has stars in her eyes as she looks between us. "Should we get a table while we wait for Biff?"

"Yes please," I say, trying to curb my laughter. While Emily talks to the hostess, I twist so I'm facing Jake. "You'd better behave,

Marty." Then something clicks in my mind, and my jaw drops as I realize why he went with that particular name. "Oh, I'm going to kill you, Jake Moody."

He bites his lip, failing to fight his smile. "No you're not. How are you feeling now?"

I feel like I want to smack him and then kiss him, or maybe just skip to the kissing part even though I'm supposed to be focusing on this business meeting and not making out with my pretend husband for the first time. Since I can't go that route, I content myself with running my fingers along his jaw and smiling up at him.

"I'm feeling like you are the best thing to ever happen to me and I'm not nervous anymore. How did you do that?"

He shrugs. "Call it a gift. People are sometimes easier to fix than computers, especially when they're willing to face their fears and be vulnerable."

"Who in the world are you?" I whisper.

He leans in and presses his forehead to mine, melting me with the sweetness of the gesture. "For now, your loving husband."

"And after that?"

"Right this way," the hostess says, breaking the spell Jake has put over me.

I wish I could have gotten an answer to my question first, but I'm not stupid enough to think I'll get to keep Jake. Not only do we live in separate states, but there's the whole matter of the FBI hunting him down. Still, there's something in the way he's looking at me that has me wondering if there's a chance we could be more than passing ships.

If nothing else, I *will* be kissing this man before the day is through.

"Let's get a picture before Biff gets here," Emily says once we reach our table. She hands a phone to the hostess and pulls herself up against me. I am more than happy to take a picture with her, only she grabs Rhys and brings him into the photo as well, and then she looks over at Jake.

Jake turns pale and looks around the restaurant. Pretending to be someone is one thing, but posing for a photo that will likely be seen by millions of people? Even without the risk of someone recognizing him, I have a feeling he's not much of a public person.

"Oh, Marty doesn't like being on the internet," I say quickly, giving Emily my best smile. "Besides, I like keeping him all to myself."

Before Emily can protest, Jake presses a kiss to my cheek and then takes her phone from the waitress, silently offering to take the picture for us.

I'm pretty sure my face is flaming red, but I smile anyway. I'll pretend I was so excited to meet Emily that I couldn't keep my emotions to myself so I don't have to admit that Jake's kiss has me reeling in the best way. The feel of his lips on my skin feels like a day at the spa, and it only makes me even more desperate to kiss him for real. I may not survive mouth-to-mouth, but I am here. for. it.

Jake's smile takes on a mischievous tilt as he snaps several photos, his eyes sliding up to meet mine. He probably knows exactly why I'm so red, and he is absolutely going to be my cause of death if he keeps smirking at me like that.

"Now just us girlies," Emily says, shoving Rhys to the side. He takes it all in stride, even smiling as he settles in his chair and waits for us to pose together.

Suddenly a thick arm slides around my shoulders, a hot body pressing up against my back as a cloud of cologne settles over me. "Looks like I'm right on time," a deep voice says.

I don't miss the way Jake stiffens and drops his smile, though I'm a little preoccupied with the fingers trailing down my upper arm. I'm generally fine with physical contact and am often the one initiating it with people I barely know, but this is taking presumption a little too far.

"Biff," Emily says through gritted teeth. "Nice to see you again."

"And you, Matisse," he says, though his face is angled toward me instead of her. "And this must be the irresistible No Man is an Isla."

I wiggle myself out from under his arm, nearly falling over as I try to navigate away from him. Thankfully, Jake reaches out to steady me, and there's a question in his eyes. "I'm fine," I whisper to him before turning around to face Biff.

He's as muscled as his photos say, though he looks a tad less impressive when he isn't all oiled. I expected him to show up in workout clothes, but he put on jeans and a short-sleeved plaid button-up. Surprising. Clearly he puts in the work and has earned his celebrity status, but I absolutely don't like the way he's taking me in from head to foot, especially when his eyes linger on the empty space where my leg should be.

"I thought the fake leg might have been a gimmick," he says, lifting an eyebrow.

Jake immediately wraps his arm around my waist as he hands Emily's phone back to her. "Hi," he says, his voice gritty and his body tense. "You must be the buff guy."

Biff scoffs. "Biff the Buff Boy," he corrects, even though that doesn't make it sound better. "Who are you?"

Jake's arm tightens around me. "I'm Marty, Isla's husband. Marty McFly."

Why did he have to add that last part? He's going to blow this whole thing by using a name from *Back to the Future* to match Biff's name, and I'm going to lose this collab opportunity because Emily is going to realize I've lied to her and Biff is going to spend the whole time hitting on me and making me wish I'd never come to Sun City.

To my utter surprise, no one reacts to the name. Outside of Rhys narrowing his eyes a little as he glances between Jake and Biff, I'm not sure if anyone even made the connection to the movie.

Biff seems more preoccupied with the *husband* part, his eyes dropping to the ring on my finger as I put my hand over Jake's.

"Dang," he says, frowning like we just told him his quick oil change is actually going to have to be an engine overhaul. "I had big plans for the two of us, Adams."

A nervous laugh ekes out of me. I'm not unused to guys flirting with me, but I think I've hit emotional overload. I'm not feeling on my game like I usually am. "Hopefully those plans are just going to look a little different," I mutter, leaning more heavily into Jake.

He must read into that lean because he grabs hold of my crutches and gestures to the closest chair. "Would you like to sit down, babe? I know you're still feeling a little sore."

I'd pretty much forgotten about all of my scrapes and bruises, and they all come back in sharp relief, stinging and aching. As I settle in the chair, I can't help but wonder how Cam and Kailani are going to react when they see me. I can probably come up with some sort of adventurous tale of how I got my injuries, but will I need to keep Jake out of it? I'm not sure I can.

Taking the chair beside me, leaving Biff to sit on his other side across from Rhys, Jake wraps his hand around mine and leans in close. "Doing okay?"

The answer to that question will depend on him. "Never leave my side."

He smiles, showing me that wildly adorable dimple. I want to kiss it so badly that I can't help but reach out and touch it, though it disappears as soon as I do. I know Jake feels the same pull between us that I do—how could he not?—but what does that mean? Is there any possible way we could see if this attraction could lead to something more when our lives are so disconnected from each other?

"How long have you two been married?" Emily asks.

I flinch. Somehow I forgot she was across from me for a second. Jake and I didn't talk about any details of our fake marriage, which was probably pretty stupid on our part. Guess I'll have to wing it.

"We got married a little over a year ago," I say with as much confidence as I can muster. I know for sure I was still crushing hard on Kit at that point because he hadn't gotten engaged yet so he was still fair game. Not really. As soon as he ran into the love of his life, Skyler, last summer, he was completely gone for her and never saw anyone else. Regardless, odds are high that I mentioned my nonexistent husband back then.

Emily hums, glancing between us. "How have you stayed in the honeymoon phase this long? It's like you've never seen each other before today."

I can't hold back my smile as I look back at Jake. Only, he isn't smiling. He looks perfectly serious as his eyes roam my face. My smile slowly fades the longer I look at him.

"Isla caught me by surprise when we met," he says gently. "And she's been surprising me ever since. I don't think it's ever possible to know every detail about a person, so I'm never going to stop being fascinated by her. And wanting to know what she loves and what she fears makes me treasure every moment I get with her. You never know how many of those moments you're going to get with someone, so I don't plan to take any of them for granted."

What in the world? Why am I *crying*?

Jake brushes away the tear that slips onto my cheek, and then he turns to the rest of the table with a smile. "Sorry. She hates when I do that, but I can't help it."

Rhys scoots closer to Emily, like he suddenly feels like he doesn't love her enough and wants to up his game.

Biff swears softly, but he's got an impressed smile on his face. "No wonder you got her attention," he says before pulling his phone out of his pocket and reading whatever message he must have just gotten.

My own phone buzzes in my lap, startling me. Without looking down, I hand it to Jake, who frowns. "I'm never going to concentrate if it keeps going off," I explain softly. "Feel free to do any research you might need to do. I have no idea how long this lunch is going to go."

That's okay. As long as he doesn't leave my side, I can make it through this.

Chapter Eight

Jake

HADLEY IS IN CUSTODY.

I didn't plan to use Isla's phone, wanting to be present for her, but as soon as she and Emily started talking about starting a new clothing line, they lost me. Rhys gave me a knowing smile and pulled up a book on his phone, which likely meant this was going to take a while, so I looked up warrants and arrest records for the day just to pass some time.

Honestly, I'm more confused than ever knowing Frank Hadley is behind bars. I'm not sure how they caught him when our setup clearly failed, and I don't want to risk digging further when I could compromise Isla's phone. According to the limited information I've found, he was caught this morning. *Hours ago.*

Where does that leave me?

News sites are still pushing the APB to find me, and they're saying Hadley still has unknown associates on the loose. Do they think I'm one of them? That I tipped Hadley off about the trap to try to...what? What in the world could I have had to gain by leaking an FBI operation and making it moot?

"Isn't that right, sweetie?" Isla says, wrapping her arm through mine.

I plaster on a smile, though I have no idea where the conversation was. "Absolutely?" It comes out to be more of a question than I'd like. I clear my throat. "Sorry, work took my attention for a bit there."

"Everything good?" Isla asks at the same time Biff says, "What keeps you busy, McFly?"

I have to try so hard not to laugh at the name. I shouldn't have used it, but by some miracle no one seems to have made the connection except maybe Rhys, who fights his own smile despite being focused on his phone. It wouldn't be so funny if Biff didn't fit his namesake so well. The antagonist in Back to the Future is a lot dumber than the real-life Biff, but they look and sound so similar that I couldn't help myself.

"I do some web design," I tell him.

Isla suddenly grows tense beside me, pulling my full attention to her. She's taken her phone back—or maybe I handed it to her—and her eyes are fixed on the multiple texts and missed calls she must have gotten while I was digging. I turned her phone to the 'do not disturb' setting, something I probably shouldn't have done.

"Everything okay?" I ask.

Isla doesn't get a chance to answer because Biff groans loudly, looking at his watch. "Dang it, I lost track of time. I've got a commercial shoot to get to, so I'll make this quick. Matisse, Adams, I'm starting up a nonprofit to help impoverished women gain autonomy and independence, and I'm thinking your collaboration is exactly what I need to get things off the ground."

The whole vibe of the table shifts, both Emily and Isla gaping at the man. Even Rhys has looked up, his eyebrows high. I'm tempted to steal Isla's phone back so I can figure out what sort of scandal he's trying to cover up by pretending to be some great humanitarian.

Isla speaks first. "You're...what?"

Biff laughs as if he knows exactly how ridiculous he sounds right now. "I know, I know. Not my usual MO. But I was raised by a single mother who worked herself to the bone trying to keep a roof over our heads because she was never given a chance to get a better job. And I know it's way worse in other parts of the world. Matisse, you're heading to Uganda tomorrow, right?"

Emily stutters through her response. "Yes, I have some contacts over there we're wanting to work with. Trying to create some jobs."

Biff turns to Isla, who is completely motionless. "And your biggest selling point of your platform is keeping costs as low as possible so anyone can purchase high quality products." He's not asking. He's stating. "The way I see it, we can all benefit each other here. I have a ground zero for starting my program, Matisse has jobs she can promise, and you, Isla, have a workforce of entry-level employees who can learn useful skills they can take to better jobs in the future."

I'm as stunned as the rest of the table—Isla looks like she's turned to stone, though I can already tell she's considering the idea—but I don't get a chance to find out how the ladies are going to respond. A niggling feeling in my belly pulls my attention to the lobby right as Agent Fields steps inside and heads for the hostess.

Crap.

"Bathroom," I choke and slip out of my seat, even though I feel sick about the idea of leaving Isla behind. I can't let her be seen with me. I move as quickly as I can without drawing attention to myself, grateful that our table is close to the kitchens so I don't have to go far. Though I lose my vest and tie the instant I'm out of sight of the lobby, it's not going to be enough of a disguise.

It's not quite four, which means the restaurant is slow enough that I don't pass any staff until I hit the breakroom, where a single employee snoozes in a hard plastic chair. Magnetic name tags hang on one wall next to a bunch of black aprons. I grab one of each, donning both before heading right back out and pausing at the edge of the hallway, just before the dining area. Do I dare look?

Yes. I need to know if Fields is here for me or if this is a crazy coincidence. How did he find me?

Poking my head around the corner, I check on Isla first. Biff is gone, and Isla and Emily are deep in discussion. Emily looks thrilled, but Isla keeps glancing toward the bathrooms. After a moment, she catches sight of me by the kitchen and frowns as soon as we make eye contact.

I grimace, wishing I had a way to explain everything from here, and then I search the room for Fields.

He's talking to the hostess and showing her something on his phone, though she seems more confused than concerned. I'm not stupid enough to think a fancy hairdo and a name tag that reads "Sean" is going to fool an FBI agent, but I am still tempted to get closer and try to overhear what he's saying. Is he looking for me? Or is he trying to decide what takeout to get for the other agents?

"Jake!"

I jump when I realize Isla is only a foot away from me, and I grab her arm before she pulls any attention our way. But I tug too hard, making her stumble, and she slips into my arms as her crutches crash at our feet. Momentum pulls us backward, spinning us until she's against the wall and caged in by my arms as I catch myself.

Her breath leaves her lungs on impact, though I don't think she hit the wall hard. "Sorry," I say as my heart pounds in my chest. I can barely breathe, though Fields is not entirely to blame for that. I hadn't planned on being trapped in a dark corridor with Isla like this.

She swallows. "Who is that out there?"

I shouldn't tell her. I should keep her out of this so she doesn't wind up in more trouble than I'm worth. But she's gazing at me with those big blue eyes of hers, and my mouth doesn't listen to my orders to stay shut.

"Agent Fields. He's the field agent that shot at me."

She gasps in alarm, but then she pulls her eyebrows low. "There's a field agent named Agent Fields?"

"Yep." This is so not the time to laugh, but I can't help it. I snort, pulling myself closer to her as she grins. It's like her smile is tied to me, and I can't resist the pull. "He didn't appreciate it when I pointed that out earlier."

"Must be why he tried to shoot you."

We both break into laughter, though I cover her mouth with my palm to keep her quiet. "This is serious, Isla," I whisper, though the closer I get to her, the more I can't remember why. Her eyes are the color of the sky on a clear summer day, something I haven't seen enough of lately. I'm always working, parked in front of a screen and forgetting that there's a real world out there. A world where people like Isla exist.

When I lower my hand, Isla licks her lips, tugging my attention to her mouth as she asks, "What do we do?"

I wish I could stay right here all day and catalog everything about her face. Every freckle and curve. "I need to figure out if he's looking for me, but I don't know how to—Isla!"

She's already hopping away and peering around the corner, but she only looks for half a second before she scrambles back to my arms and says, "Kiss me."

"What?" I choke on the word.

But instead of clarifying, Isla grabs me by the collar and tugs my head down until our lips crash together.

I may have no clue what her plan is, but I follow her orders to the letter. Her mouth is warm and pliant and tastes slightly of the garlic chicken she ordered for lunch, and I can't get enough. Isla kisses with passion and hunger, which I match with enthusiasm. My hands find her waist and pull her flush against me at the same time she thrusts her fingers into the hair at the back of my neck, and goosebumps erupt across my skin as she parts her lips to invite me in. I've never kissed anyone like this before, and I'm sure I never will again. It's fire and weightlessness and the feeling of nothing ever going wrong as long as we're connected like this.

My brain registers some sort of sound in the hazy distance, but I don't care. All I care about is kissing Isla.

But she jerks away from me and forces my head down into her chest. Not that I'm complaining, but... "Do you mind?" she says, sounding as breathless as I feel.

My body, which a moment ago had been filled with molten lava, turns to ice when a gruff voice replies, "Excuse me. I'm looking for this man. Have you seen him? He was recently in the area."

Isla hums, still holding my head down against her body. "I don't think so. But I've been a little preoccupied. My husband's breaks are so short, so we try to make the most of them." Her fingers run through my hair, making me shudder with pleasure. No one has ever done that before. At least, not the way she does it.

"Sir?" Fields clears his throat. "I need to ask you some questions."

I groan, knowing I can't hide my face in Isla's chest forever. The minute I lift my head, Fields is going to recognize me and arrest us both.

"Excuse me, what's going on?" An unfamiliar voice enters the fray, and she sounds more than a little annoyed. "Your break ended five minutes ago. Table three needs more bread."

"On it," I say and pull away from Isla, keeping my head down to avoid both Fields and the woman behind me.

"Hey!" Fields shouts, but I don't look back, hoping my new manager keeps him occupied long enough for me to slip out the back.

Chapter Nine

Isla

MAYBE IT'S A BAD idea, but when I get back to the table, I tell Emily and Rhys that my husband got food poisoning and headed out. Emily tells me I should go with him, but I know I need to stick around so Agent Fields doesn't get more suspicious than he already is.

Honestly, I'm amazed my idea worked and that Jake managed to get away, though a lot of the credit goes to the young shift lead, Kinley, who unknowingly helped by telling Fields that he couldn't wander around bothering patrons without a warrant. I'm not sure if that's how it works, but Fields seemed to realize he wasn't going to get any cooperation and instead sat himself at a table, probably to wait for "Sean" to come back out.

I really hope Jake is smart enough to find a back door or something.

"Marty will be okay," I tell Emily, forcing a smile. "He took an Uber back to the hotel, and he didn't want me to waste any time I get with you."

I can feel Fields glancing at me every so often, so I try to relax even though my hand is shaking as I reach for my glass of water. I would say it's only fear and adrenaline making me tremble, but that would be an utter lie.

I am never going to recover from that kiss.

Though in reality it lasted only a few seconds, it felt like an eternity, and my lips are still tingling. I didn't even know it was possible for a kiss to feel that electric. That momentous. That *life-changing*. I may have caught Jake by surprise when I kissed him, but the joke was on me because I never could have expected a kiss like that, so full of fire that I would have melted into the floor if he hadn't been holding on to me so tightly. I knew a kiss with Jake was going to be good, but that was the kiss I will forever compare all kisses to.

"Isla?"

I jolt in my seat, blinking hard as I struggle to focus on Emily. "Sorry, what?"

She gives me a sympathetic smile as Rhys waves down our waitress. "I know we planned to spend all afternoon together, but you really can go take care of Marty. I'm sure he would love to have you by his side."

I am desperate to go outside and find him, but half of me is still focused on the real reason I'm here. Before Biff left, he promised to email us all of his proposals for his nonprofit to prove that he's serious, and my gut tells me that I should believe him. Emily said she feels the same way, which means we've got something big in front of us.

I slump in my chair, hating that I'm so torn. "You're going to Africa in the morning," I remind her. "And I needed to make plans for my winter releases, like, a month ago. I know it was risky and presumptuous of me to bank on this collaboration, but—"

"I have a crazy idea," Emily says, grabbing my hand. "Before you say anything, hear me out, okay?"

I usually love crazy ideas, and yesterday this conversation would have pumped me up, even without knowing where Emily is going with this. But yesterday I didn't know Jake, and it feels like everything in my life has shifted and left me off balance.

I should be used to that, but this is different.

"Talk crazy to me," I tell Emily weakly.

She gives my hand a squeeze. "Come to Uganda with me."

"What?"

"Just listen. You and I both know if this thing with Biff is real, it could be huge for all of us. But even if it isn't, can you imagine what the two of us could do if we set up a factory together? You could teach the women how to sew your products so the training wouldn't cost you anything but time, and I can get you enough media attention to get pre-orders going so we can start paying good wages with or without Biff's nonprofit. We could do so much good, Isla, and you can finally branch out from athleticwear and design something you actually love."

It's not that I hate athleticwear, and I've truly loved being able to build up my company like I have. But I don't think I realized how much more I want to do until Emily voiced my feelings for me just now.

"Think about it," Emily pleads. "Besides, it would be nice to have another woman there with me. Rhys is great, but I need my gal pals."

I glance at Rhys, who shrugs. Seriously, he's like the perfect husband and seems to do whatever Emily wants him to do, but he also seems happy to be that way.

I know I shouldn't, but I can't help but wonder how Jake would be as a husband. An actual husband.

"I'll need to talk it over with Marty," I say, holding back a grimace. Suddenly I don't like lying to Emily about who Jake is.

Rhys clears his throat. "His last name isn't really McFly, is it?"

I let out a shaky laugh. "No. He was messing with Biff."

"Oh, that's a relief," Emily says while her husband chuckles. "That would have been the most unfortunate name. If he works in web design, would he be able to come with you? Whenever we go, we rent out a huge house, and there would be plenty of room for you both. Rhys has a home office he'd be happy to share with Marty."

She must really want me there, and I really want to go with her. She's right when she says this could be huge for us, and I've never left the country even though I've always wanted to travel and have my passport ready to go.

But Jake coming with me? There's a large and frustrated FBI agent a few tables away that makes that feel impossible. More likely than not, Jake will be caught sooner than later, and who knows what will happen to him?

"I should go," I say, fully aware of the misery in my voice. "Let me think about Uganda, and we'll get in touch once you're settled." It's only then that I realize Rhys already paid the check. "Oh no, I was going to pay for lunch!"

Emily waves me away. "You drove all the way to Sun City. It's the least I can do. I really hope you come to Africa, Isla, but I understand if you can't. Now go. Take care of that scrumptious husband of yours."

She doesn't have to tell me twice, though I'm still a little leery of the agent nearby. He's ordering food and seems to have given up his search, though, so I try not to look nervous as I hug Emily and then make my way to the front door and outside into the sun. As long as Agent Fields stays inside long enough for me to find Jake and get as far from the restaurant as we can, I can—

"Isla."

Jake steps out from behind a bush, still wearing the apron and name tag, and relief washes over me. Dropping my crutches, I throw my arms around him, pulling myself in tight.

"You're okay," I breathe at the same time he asks, "Are you okay?" Jake holds me so tightly that I can barely breathe, but I don't want him to let go.

I have ten siblings, one of whom is an active duty Marine, and a mom who gets frequent panic attacks and a dad who teaches Driver's Ed. Yet I've never been this worried about another person, and I'm terrified of what that means. How can I care so deeply for a person I've only known for six hours?

"I'm fine," I say when I realize how tense Jake is. "I think Field Agent Fields is tired of hunting you and just wants a hot meal now."

Finally loosening his hold, Jake glances at the restaurant. His expression keeps shifting, slowly growing more and more miserable, and I don't like where his thoughts are going.

"No," I say as forcefully as I can.

He grimaces and takes a step away from me, though I grab his hand before he can get too far. "Isla."

"You can't turn yourself in!"

"This isn't going to end until I'm caught. You know that."

"No, I don't know that. I don't know anything about what's going to happen to you. I hate that." And now I'm crying, which would be annoying except it convinces Jake to wrap me up in his arms again. Is this the last time I'll ever be able to hug him?

Sighing, Jake presses his hand to my head like he wants to protect me from the world. "I wish I could have found some answers," he says gently, stroking my hair. "Honestly, I have no idea what's going to happen either, but as long as you're okay, I'll—"

Pulling myself free, I grab his neck and tug his mouth to mine. Jake responds immediately, just like last time. This kiss is no less electric than the last, but unlike then, this one feels like a goodbye kiss. If that's what this is going to be, I'm not going to waste a moment of it. I let my hands roam, exploring his hair, his shoulders, his chest—anywhere I can reach. Jake's hands burn against my hips, pressing into my skin through the fabric of my dress as he matches my desire beat for beat.

When Jake slows our kisses, I know we're almost at the end, but I'm not ready to say goodbye. How am I supposed to just drive back to Diamond Springs and carry on with my life as if he was never in it? Sure, I could go on the journey of a lifetime and join Emily in Africa, but now that I know it's possible to feel this strongly about a person, I'm not sure I'll ever recover.

Brushing my tears from my cheeks, Jake presses his forehead to mine and takes a shaky breath. "I've never known anyone like you, Isla Adams. You're going to change the world, one pair of pants at a time."

"And you're going to save it," I whisper back, burying my face in his chest. "Promise me you'll be okay."

He doesn't say a word, and I don't blame him.

But someone else chooses to fill the silence for him. "Uh, Isla?"

I stiffen. I know that voice. And now I know what all those texts and voicemails on my phone probably say.

Still clinging to Jake like my life depends on him, I slowly turn to face my brother-in-law. Only, it's not just Cam standing there with his massive arms folded across his chest. Kit is next to him, his eyes narrowed on Jake, while their other two friends, Ben and Oliver, stand near Cam's car as if unsure what to do about the situation. I don't blame them. The Wonder Boys, as they call themselves, have never been in a situation quite like this.

"This is a rescue," Ben says after several seconds of tense silence.

Oliver smirks, leaning one shoulder against the car. "Though, it doesn't seem like you're in as much danger as Superman here seems to think."

"Shut up, Hamilton," Cam barks, eyes still locked on me. "Why didn't you answer your phone, Isla?"

I hate when he gets all menacing like this. He's already huge and insanely strong, and though he's a teddy bear beneath all the bulk, my brother-in-law can look genuinely terrifying. I grab Jake's hand, just in case he's feeling the animosity as much as I am. "Kailani didn't come with you?"

Cam clenches his jaw. He knows I'm not afraid of him, but I am terrified of disappointing my sister. He hates that he can't get to me like she does.

"She got a flat tire and sent us on ahead," Oliver explains when Cam doesn't answer my question. "I wonder what we would have interrupted if we'd stayed to help and come ten minutes later."

"Oliver," Kit warns, grabbing Cam's arm before he can turn on Oliver. They're friends, but sometimes Cam and Oliver really get on each other's nerves. "Isla, are you okay?"

All four men look at Jake, who shrinks beside me.

I roll my eyes, squeezing Jake's hand. "I'm fine, Kit. Just like I texted Cam earlier today."

"You call swapping spit with a *terrorist* fine?" Cam says. Then he turns his glare to Jake. "You'd better get your filthy paws off her or I'll—"

"Cam!" I shout, but I'm not the only one shouting.

A rough voice growls, "Moody!" right before a big body tackles Jake, tearing him out of my grip and knocking me off balance.

I crash to the ground, but I barely feel the impact because all of my focus is on Jake as Agent Fields hauls him to his feet and drags him away. Not that Jake is fighting him. The Wonder Boys swarm me, helping me up, and I curse my missing leg for making it too difficult for me to chase after Jake. If only I could explain that he's not the bad guy, that he helped me, that he's been nothing but the best man I've ever known.

If only I could tell Jake that I'm pretty sure I'm falling in love with him.

Fields stuffs Jake into the back of an SUV and slams the door, and I get one last glimpse of his beautiful face through the window before he's gone.

Chapter Ten
Jake

"What in the world are you doing on the floor?"

I keep my eyes closed despite the annoyed question. Holding this meditative yoga pose is the only thing that has kept me breathing over the last three hours as I've sat in this holding room by myself, waiting to hear my fate. I'm surprised they didn't take me straight to a cell, but I suppose there's a procedure they have to follow.

"Mr. Moody, I've already had a hellish day. Would you mind sitting in a chair like a normal human?"

I finally open one eye, recognizing the agent as one of the ones at the park this morning. He was in the van.

I don't move.

The agent sighs and takes one of the chairs that sits on either side of the metal desk in the middle of the room. He's older than I expected, his hair a mix of white and gray, and he's full of tension. "I'm Agent Van Park."

I open my other eye. Now I'm more than a little convinced that all of these names are fake. Agent Fields, Agent Van Park, Agent Waites. (He was the one who took me to this holding room. Where I've been waiting.)

Van Park gestures to the chair, trying one more time to get me off the floor, but gives up when I don't budge. "Your choice," he says, clasping his hands together. "We've been looking all over for you today, Mr. Moody."

I should probably claim my right to a lawyer, but I don't know if that would actually help or just make me look guilty. I am more than happy to remain silent and keep trying to breathe. It isn't easy, knowing I didn't get to give Isla a proper goodbye beyond that kiss that left my body burning. I'll likely never see her again, and this dark void in my chest where she spent the day is only going to grow bigger.

"You could have saved us a lot of trouble," Van Park continues. "I'm not sure why you thought it was a good idea to run, but my agents have been scouring this city for hours trying to find you."

Does he think I don't know that? I close my eyes and concentrate on taking a deep breath, holding it in my lungs for a few seconds before slowly releasing it. I've been trying not to hear Isla's voice in my head telling me to breathe. I've been failing.

"Oh, so we couldn't get you to shut up earlier, and now we can't get a word out of you?"

I open my eyes again. "You haven't asked me a question."

Van Park doesn't flinch. "Yes, I have. I asked what you were doing on the floor."

"Yoga."

"Why?"

"Because it helps in stressful situations."

"We could have avoided most of this stress if you had just done as you were told."

Some of my careful calm slips as I stare at him. "Your guy tried to shoot me!"

Van Park barks a laugh as if I just said one of the funniest jokes he's heard all year. "Shoot you! You can't even imagine the kind of paperwork that would entail. Fields didn't try to shoot you."

I clench my hands into fists on my knees. "I was there. You know, the one staring down the barrel of his gun? I'm lucky he missed."

"Fields is one of our best shots," Van Park argues. "He didn't miss."

I gesture to my body, which is free of bullet holes, as far as I can tell.

Van Park twists in his seat so he can rest his head in his hand, and he grins down at me like he's never had this much fun. "You're a smart kid, Jake. I like that about you. But you're also an idiot."

I force my gaze to the floor and clench my jaw again. I need to be smart and not antagonize the man who holds my life in his hands. "This feels like excessive force," I grumble, knowing I should really shut my mouth.

"Does it? I think Frank Hadley would rather be in your position. He's the one that got shot."

My head snaps up. "What?"

Van Park chuckles. "Honestly, you should be glad Fields agreed to keep an eye on you 'cause he saved your life."

"Saved my...?" I'm feeling dizzy, and it takes me a second to realize I'm not breathing. I choke down some air and unfold myself as I try to understand. "Fields saved my life...by shooting Frank Hadley?"

Van Park nods. "Hadley was smart when he picked that spot. Not great visibility from that south side, with all that foliage blocking the street. We're not sure yet what tipped him off or if he planned to take you out from the beginning, but you're lucky Fields caught sight of Hadley just in time. But then you had to go and run away. Do you have any idea how hard it is to protect someone who lives off the grid like you do?"

Oh, this is making my head hurt. "The news," I mutter. "You put an APB out on me. Why did you say I was dangerous?"

"People pay better attention to stuff like that." Van Park says it like it should be obvious. "They wouldn't care if we told them you were *in* danger. For the record, we only said that you *might* be dangerous. Not that you are."

"But calling me a cyber terrorist?"

He lets out a wheezy laugh. "That was an unfortunate misunderstanding. Someone looked deeper and found that piece of your history. They're not running the story anymore, if you'd care to know, though there's only so much we can do about anyone who has shared that info."

"Yes, that makes me feel *so* much better," I growl, rising to my feet. Now that the truth is starting to sink in, my misery is turning into frustration. "You let me run around the city thinking my freedom and my life were in danger, and you couldn't find a way to tell me that you were just trying to keep me safe?"

I hate that Van Park isn't fazed by my anger in the slightest. "How would you have liked me to get in touch with you?" he says lightly. "Your credit card slip up at that pawn shop was the only reason we knew which area to start looking."

Okay, he makes a good point there.

"And in all reality, you *were* a cyber terrorist."

I groan. "You were just waiting to say that, weren't you?"

"We all know you've turned your life around, Moody, though we're still going to be wary of you for a while. Honestly, we never would have found Hadley without your help, so that has earned you some points. Plus, now we know how to find you."

Something I'm not especially fond of.

"So can I go?" If I'm lucky, Isla hasn't left town yet, though I'm not sure I'll be able to get past her bodyguards even if she is still in Sun City. I have no idea who those men were, but they clearly care about her. Even if I have to fight my way through them, it would be worth it for a chance to hold Isla in my arms again.

"About that," Van Park says, preemptively flinching as if he knows I'm not going to like what he's about to say. "We need to keep you in custody for a few days. Maybe a week."

"*A week*? But you said—"

"I didn't say anything about letting you go, Moody. You didn't follow orders, and you caused a whole lot of trouble with your disappearing act today."

"Tell me what crime I committed, and we can talk about custody," I snarl, slamming my hands on the table.

Van Park doesn't move. Apparently his momentary fear of me was just that. Momentary. "Then there's the matter of Hadley's associates. We can't in good conscience let you out there without knowing how many there are and if they're going to be after you."

Yesterday, I would have told him I couldn't care less about the danger, but today I keep my mouth shut. If something happens to me, it'll affect Isla too. I'm not so vain to think she's in love with me, but I know she'd be hurt if something happened to me. She cares. I don't know to what degree, but she feels something between us just like I do. I can't bear to risk that.

"A week?" I repeat, slowly sinking into the other chair.

He nods. "Give us that, and then we'll talk."

It's a week that I'll have to wait to get a bus ticket to go see Isla in Diamond Springs, but as long as I can explain the situation, I hope she can be patient. Now that I'm not on the run—now that a future together isn't out of the question—we need to have a conversation.

"Can I—"

"No." Van Park shakes his head. "No contact with the outside world. We need Hadley's associates to think you're truly in custody, or they'll disappear for good. You found them once; you could find them again." Before I can argue that that's a great reason to give me access to the internet, he grunts and rises to his feet. "I know it sucks, Moody, but we've had to pivot from the original plan after the way things went down this morning. It's just the way it is."

"A week?" I say one more time, feeling more desperate now.

He frowns as he heads for the door. "Then we'll talk."

I really don't like the sound of that.

Chapter Eleven

Isla

July 13

"ARE YOU SURE YOU'VE packed everything you need?"

Kailani isn't usually this mothering with me, but I think she knows how big this is. I'm spending the next three months in another country, on my own for the first time in my life. Sure, Emily and Rhys will be there, but they're not my family.

"Maybe we should go through your suitcase one more time," Lani says, reaching for the nearest bag as we both sit on my bed.

"I'm going to be late for my flight," I warn her, though my voice trembles. I haven't lived more than a hallway away from my big sister since the day I was adopted, and I didn't realize how much I would hate the thought of being so far from her. She's always been there for me, but if I follow through with this Africa plan, I'll be completely on my own.

Kailani must pick up on my anxiety because she wraps her arms around me in a fierce hug. She's never been touchy-feely like this with me, but I'm not complaining. "Isla, you don't have to go. If you're not ready for something like this…"

When am I ever going to be ready for something like this? I got all the immunizations I needed, and Emily got me a killer deal on a flight, and everything is packed. But this fear isn't going to go away whether I leave now or six months from now. There's really only one thing that would make this easier. "I wish…" I'm almost too afraid to voice my thoughts out loud. "I wish Jake was going with me."

Stiffening, Kailani pulls back and studies me. I told her everything that happened in Sun City, but I'm not sure she ever believed how deeply I feel about Jake. It's been more than two weeks, and I haven't heard a word from him. Makes sense, if he's locked up in federal prison, but I asked Oliver to look up what happened to him.

Oliver is a computer guy, like Jake, but he said he couldn't find a trace of Jake Moody. Not even in all those news stories that were floating around while I was in New Mexico. Any mention of him has disappeared.

It's like Jake never existed.

Kailani takes my hand. "I know you liked him, Isla, but—"

"I think I loved him, Lani."

She frowns. "You only knew him for a few hours."

"You knew Cam less than that before you almost kissed him," I argue.

"Kissing a guy doesn't mean you love him."

I know that. I've kissed enough men to know that. But this ache in my chest? The one that hasn't gone away since opening my trunk at the restaurant and seeing my prosthesis waiting for me? Jake must have bought my leg when I went to the drugstore for hair gel, and seeing it nestled amongst my clothes hit me like a pound of bricks.

This feeling is more than a little crush.

"You ready to go?" Cam appears in the doorway, glancing between us as if he knows something heavy is in the air. He can probably feel it, though it could also be my tears that tipped him off. "Or are you going to stay here with us where it's safe?"

That comment spurs me to life, pushing me off the bed and to my feet. My artificial leg sits heavy beneath me, like it has since putting it back on the first time, but I'm so glad I have it. So glad that Jake gave up so much to get it for me. I don't know if that's how the feds found him, but I'm sure the purchase didn't help him. If nothing else, it cost him ten thousand dollars, and no money in the world can repay his kindness.

Grabbing my backpack and slipping it over my shoulders, I glare at Cam. "I'm going," I tell him, leaving no room for argument.

He holds up his hands. "Okay, you're going. We'd better hurry if you don't want to miss your flight."

I'm waiting for my connecting flight in the JFK airport, which will take me to Lagos and then to the Entebbe International Airport, when the message comes in.

I get messages from strangers all the time, but this one comes straight to my primary Instagram inbox even though it's a person I don't follow. Usually those go to my request box where they can sit until I'm brave enough to see what nonsense might be in the message. The sheer number of men who offer to be my sugar daddy is astounding. But this message...

j4752mm: Is this where you spend all your time?

I frown before glancing at my gate to make sure boarding hasn't started yet. Usually, I delete this kind of message, but instinct makes me pause. I'm not sure why.

Another message comes in before I can think of some sort of response.

j4752mm: I'm just now realizing how creepy that message sounds. Sorry. You can blame it on me spending the last two and a half weeks in an FBI bunker with no one but Agent Fields to keep me company.

My heart picks up its pace. It can't be...

Me: Jake?
j4752mm: Hi.

Me: You have an Instagram?

j4752mm: I do now. It felt safer than getting a phone, though I'm not sure I trust the security claims from Zuckerberg. I'm at the library right now, and I only have a few minutes before this person is logged out. At least the librarian can't accuse me of doing anything illegal right now.

It really is him! My chest swells with relief, and tears fill my eyes as I hug my phone like it might get me closer to him. My phone buzzes with another message, and I wipe my eyes before looking down.

j4752mm: I know my timing is terrible. I'm not going to stop you from joining Emily, but I wanted to make sure you were okay after everything that happened.

I almost ask how he knows I'm going to Uganda, but then I remember who I'm talking to. He probably knows that I'm sitting in an airport terminal and wearing Crocs because they're so comfortable for traveling. If my brother-in-law can track my phone to find me at a restaurant in the next state over, a reformed cyber criminal can look up my whereabouts. And my Instagram stories, I guess. I haven't been shy about telling my followers my plans.

I type out a message but hesitate before sending it. Do I want to say what's on my mind?

Me: I miss you.

Maybe that's too forward, but I've been missing him for weeks. And having this screen between us is making me feel bold. Luckily, his next message fills me with warmth.

j4752mm: You have no idea how much I miss you, Isla Adams.

j4752mm: I tried to escape a couple of times to get to you, but Fields is too good at his job. He was convinced I would be axed as soon as I set foot outside even though I told him I would be fine. But I decided it's too hard to be in love on the run, so I let him run the show so he wouldn't try to arrest me or something. I want to be able to love you freely.

OH. Okay, so I'm not the only one who thinks what we had was love? *Take that, Kailani!* Wait, he *loves* me?

As if he can read me from across the country, Jake sends another message.

j4752mm: Yes, I love you, Isla. Desperately. I've had a hole in my chest since the moment they took me away from you, and I had a lot of time to think about you while I was under protection. I wanted you to know how I feel while you're off changing lives. You know, in case you ever come back.

j4752mm: I would come with you if the feds didn't tell me I would be branded a terrorist again if I try to leave the country. I'm inclined to do what they say for a while.

Me: I'll be back in October.

Me: And I love you too Jake.

j4752mm: I'll be here waiting.

Chapter Twelve

July 19

nomanisanisla: Mbale is amazing! Emily has been showing me around the city this week, and the people are so welcoming. So many of the women here are excited to start work immediately, and some of them are even going to help me with some designs while I'm here. There's a little boy here who is obsessed with our office computer. He reminds me a lot of you, but I think he might be cuter than you. He told me he would marry me when he's old enough, and I told him we would talk about it in fifteen years. He looked so excited! Don't worry. You're the only computer nerd for me. XOXO

July 20

j4752mm: I met a guy at a diner yesterday who looked like he had hit rock bottom. I looked him up, and apparently there was some big scandal with his company and his partner lost people millions of dollars. Poor guy. I was going to give him some money and carry on my way, but then I thought "what would Isla do?" I offered him my spare bedroom instead, and he looked at me like I was crazy. It's probably because I've taken up knitting while I wait for you to come home. (It's the only thing keeping me from making a fake passport and following you to Uganda.) I was wearing my first attempt at a shirt, and it looks terrible. But the guy said yes, so I'm going to have a new roommate in a few days. He's so uptight that I'm going to need to find a way to get under his skin and help him breathe. Good thing someone taught me how to do that. I love you. I miss you. Please don't fall in love with any nerds unless they're me.

July 28

nomanisanisla: We invited a bunch of kids over for a movie night last night, and you'll never guess what movie Rhys put on for them.

nomanisanisla: Okay, you can probably guess. It's one you've seen.

nomanisanisla: No guesses?

nomanisanisla: I forgot about the time difference again. I hope you're sleeping right now!

j4752mm: Back to the Future.

nomanisanisla: Why are you awake?

j4752mm: Because you messaged me.

nomanisanisla: Ooooo sorry!

j4752mm: Never be sorry for sending me messages. It lets me know I'm on your mind almost as much as you're on mine.

nomanisanisla: *heart emoji*

nomanisanisla: How do you get my messages anyway? Did you finally get a phone?

j4752mm: Ha! No. Laptop. But I'm pretending I don't have it because my roommate is starting to think I'm some hippie weirdo who doesn't trust technology, and it's driving him nuts.

nomanisanisla: What's his name? And do you like having a roommate?

j4752mm: Are you asking because you'd like to be my roommate? I'll gladly trade him for you.

nomanisanisla: Jacob Moody!

j4752mm: His name is Fischer, and he is the most tense person I've ever met. He needs a serious reset.

nomanisanisla: Like an aura cleanse!

j4752mm: A what?

nomanisanisla: Look it up. I'm too busy blushing from your roommate comment.

j4752mm: Because it's true, right? You would LOVE to be my roommate.

j4752mm: By the way, I am not responsible for any messages I send while half asleep.

nomanisanisla: Go back to sleep, Jake.

nomanisanisla: And yes, it's true.

j4752mm: I love you.

August 16

nomanisanisla: You kept me up way too late with that phone call last night, Marty McFly. I feel like I'm going to fall asleep at my sewing machine which is bad because we're starting our first run of dresses today so I need to be on my game.

j4752mm: I'm sorry. Still trying to figure out my best work schedule so I can be in line with yours. Next time I won't keep you on the line so long.

nomanisanisla: I didn't say you should do that. I love hearing your voice. It makes me feel closer to home.

j4752mm: Still feeling homesick?

nomanisanisla: I've only been here a month. How am I going to last two more? Emily said she felt this way the first time she came out here and that I should lose myself in the work, but I can't stop thinking about how many miles are between me and you.

j4752mm: 8959 miles.

j4752mm: Not that I've mapped it out or anything.

nomanisanisla: I miss you like crazy. What if I just come home?

j4752mm: As much as I want to buy you a plane ticket right now and get you back in my arms where you belong, you'll regret it if you don't see this through. You've got this, Isla.

nomanisanisla: You really think I can do this?

j4752mm: I'm pretty sure you can do anything.

nomanisanisla: I love you.

j4752mm: I miss you.

j4752mm: Uganda will be better for knowing you, just like I am.

September 2

nomanisanisla: Biff showed up this morning.

j4752mm: And you're just telling me this now?

nomanisanisla: When he found out you weren't here with me, he asked me out to dinner.

nomanisanisla: Jake?

j4752mm: Sorry, just figuring out how long it will take to get that fake passport put together. There's a flight leaving Sun City tonight, and I can be there in thirty-four hours, give or take.

nomanisanisla: Don't you dare. I love you, but I'm not going to date a criminal.

j4752mm: I'm kidding. Mostly. What did you tell him?

nomanisanisla: I flashed my ring and told him I have a video date with my husband tonight.

j4752mm: You still have it?

nomanisanisla: Of course I do.

j4752: *picture of his ring*

nomanisanisla: Aww, you kept yours too!

j4752mm: Always.

j4752mm: I am and always will be yours.

September 18

j4752mm: The watch on the leg thing was genius. Fischer officially thinks I'm crazy, but he keeps trying to figure me out. The more weird things I do, the more he seems to relax.

nomanisanisla: Does he still think your name is Kale?

j4752mm: Of course he does.

nomanisanisla: That is the stupidest name.

j4752mm: There is no way I'm telling a guy like him my real name. If he's smart enough to figure out the letters are right next to the real ones, then he can earn that right. Until then, he'll just have to keep trying to avoid me because I freak him out.

nomanisanisla: Your roomie needs a girlfriend pronto. Someone who isn't afraid to loosen him up a bit. He likes girls, right?

j4752mm: I think so. Hard to tell with him, though.

nomanisanisla: I want to meet this guy so bad.

j4752mm: 36 more days and you can.

j4752mm: Unless you fall in love with Uganda and never want to come back.

nomanisanisla: I have totally fallen in love with Uganda, but it's nothing compared to how I feel about you. Any idea when that travel ban will be lifted?

j4752mm: I'm not holding my breath.

nomanisanisla: One of these days you're going to tell me what you did when you were a cyber terrorist to make the FBI so afraid of you.

j4762mm: Don't hold your breath. *winky face*

October 9

j4752mm: FISCHER MET A GIRL.

nomanisanisla: WHAT?!?!

j4752mm: He's in his room texting her right now and it's like he's a completely different person.

nomanisanisla: I KNEW IT! I told you he just needed to find himself a girlfriend!

j4752mm: He's going to mess this up. You know he is.

nomanisanisla: We need to help him!

j4752mm: How??

nomanisanisla: You're still hacked into his phone, right?

j4752mm: I can't believe you just used that word.

j4752mm: But yes.

nomanisanisla: Please tell me he's not being all stiff in his texts like he is in real life.

j4752mm: I'm surprised to say it, but he's flirting.

nomanisanisla: Fischer can flirt?

j4752mm: Apparently. Micah is doing all the heavy lifting, though. Whoever she is, Fischer is no match for her.

nomanisanisla: You're going to look her up, right?

j4752mm: Uh. Wasn't planning to.

nomanisanisla: You should! Find her in person and see if she's the right fit for our boy. I don't want Fischer to get hurt again.

j4752mm: I think I regret telling you about him.

nomanisanisla: No you don't.

j4752mm: No, I don't. I love you, Isla. If I go on a date with Micah, it doesn't mean anything.

nomanisanisla: I know. I trust you.

nomanisanisla: Only two more weeks before my flight lands in Sun City!

j4752mm: I'm counting down the days.

Chapter Thirteen
Jake

October 24

I SHOULDN'T BE THIS nervous. I've spent the last three months talking non-stop with Isla, so it's not like I don't know she's excited to see me. But computers and phone calls aren't the same as being with a person, and something could have changed over the last seven hours during her flight from Boston.

I know that's stupid of me, but the nerves are still there.

Honestly, I think being apart was good for us. We've been able to get to know each other without heightened emotions or physical chemistry distracting us. I don't know about Isla, but these last three months have made me more certain than ever that she and I were meant to find each other.

I probably should have brought a phone with me, but they're so much harder to mask than computers, so I just have to hope Isla can find me as I wait in the pickup line at the Sun City airport. I tried to time things right so I can wait here instead of circling around, but the airport attendant is starting to eye me with frustration because I've been idling here too long, standing against the hood of the car I rented for the day. Just one more minute, and then I'll make a loop, but I don't want Isla to have any reason to think I'm not—

"Jake!"

My heart jumps into my throat at the sight of Isla running toward me looking a hundred times more beautiful than I remember. She has sent hundreds of pictures, but none of them compare to the woman who drops her bags and launches herself at me.

I hold her as tightly as I can, barely believing she's actually in my arms.

"Are you crying?" she asks with a laugh.

"You're one to talk," I reply. She's shaking from her tears. "I don't think I can ever let you go."

"Maybe you can let me breathe?"

Reluctantly, I set her on her feet and take a step back so I can really get a good look at her. She's still as fair-skinned as ever, though she has more freckles than she did before, and her eyes are bright and glistening as she takes me in. Even in her sweats and t-shirt, she's the most breathtaking sight I've ever seen.

"It's really you?" she whispers, reaching up and stroking my jaw.

I can barely find my voice. "It's really *you*."

"Are you going to kiss me?"

She doesn't have to ask twice. I bend down and capture her lips with mine, losing myself in the taste of her and the feel of her in my arms.

At least until the airport attendant rudely interrupts us and tells us we need to move the car or get towed.

Once Isla's luggage is stowed in the trunk and we're on our way back into the city, my emotions start to settle, leaving me in a cloud of peace. I've never felt so content in my life, and I know this feeling is all thanks to Isla. She's here. She's safe. She's *here*.

"So," Isla says, taking off her prosthesis so she can twist in her seat to face me. "What's the update with Fischer? Did he ever respond about dinner with her family?"

I groan. "No. And he's been in Santa Fe all morning."

"Why?"

"No idea. His parents are there, but I don't think he's ever been close with them."

"How's Micah doing with the silence?"

I laugh and lace my fingers through hers. I love that we can pick up where we left off, both in terms of physicality and the conversation we were having during her last layover. "I don't have access to Micah's phone, remember?"

"I think you missed an opportunity when you took her to dinner, McFly."

I laugh, shaking my head at this ridiculous woman beside me. "I think I was a little distracted trying to figure out how to get her and Fischer together, per *your* request, I'll remind you."

Isla gasps. "I can't help that you got me invested! Where are we going, anyway?"

"My apartment. I only get you for two days before your sister is expecting you to be flying home, and I plan on keeping you all to myself."

"Wait, *Jake Moody* is showing me where he lives? What an honor!"

"The FBI know now too, so don't feel too special."

"Yeah, but you chose to tell me. So I feel incredibly special."

As I lift her hand to my lips, I can't help but grin like an idiot. It has been less than four months since the day I ran into Isla Adams. I've collectively spent six hours in her physical presence. There is no logical reason for me to trust her, and yet she has completely infiltrated my life and changed me for the better.

Her soft fingers find my cheek, and it takes all my concentration to focus on the road in front of me. "I've missed this dimple," she says on a sigh. "I've missed *you*."

Thank goodness we're nearly to my apartment because I am ready to kiss this woman senseless.

When I finally park outside my building, Isla starts putting her leg back on, but I hurry around to her door and stop her. "No time," I growl, lifting her into my arms and heading for the stairs.

"But my luggage!" she says, laughing.

"We'll get it later."

I have some lost time to make up for.

Isla

"I never want to leave this spot." I close my eyes, focusing on the lazy circles Jake draws on my arm. Though this is the most comfortable I've ever been, snuggled up together on his couch, I refuse to let myself fall asleep. The flights back to the States were brutal, but I'm hoping jetlag keeps me on Jake's same schedule while I'm here so we don't lose any time.

I still can't believe the man started working nights so he could be awake the same time I was.

Jake presses a kiss to the top of my head. We've spent the last couple of hours kissing like there's no tomorrow, but there's something about this gentle touch of his lips that feels like it's so much bigger than anything we've done before. "You could stay, you know."

His words bring a warmth to my belly that feels like something I want to cling to forever. But I can't. "You know I need to go back to Colorado."

"I know."

We've talked a lot about my family, how things used to be strained between my parents and me and have only recently gotten to a good place. It was hard enough to leave my family for a few months. Especially Kailani. "But I'll come visit whenever I can. I'll need to come work with Emily sometimes anyway, and it's only a couple of hours away."

Jake wraps his arms around me and squeezes tight, like he's afraid I might run away as he says, "I have another idea."

He sounds so nervous that I can't help but smile, wishing I could see his face but unwilling to move from this spot until I have to. "I love ideas."

"What if I move to Diamond Springs?"

I sit up, spinning to face him. "What?"

He gives me a sheepish smile. "My company is almost fully remote now anyway, and as long as I tell the FBI where I'm going, I don't see why it would cause any problems if I made a change of residence. Hadley's trial will be happening soon, and hopefully after he and his associates are officially behind bars, I won't be a point of interest anymore. I can start living a normal life again."

Oh, he has no idea how much I love what he's saying right now, but I'm trying not to freak out until it's a sure thing. "What about Fischer?"

He chuckles. "Fischer will be fine. Micah will take care of him."

"How do you know? He still hasn't replied to—"

The front door suddenly flies open, bringing a tall, dark, and handsome man into the front room, though he doesn't stop to chat. He heads straight down the hall to the bedrooms, shutting a door behind him.

I turn to Jake with wide eyes, glad to see him grinning. "Was that...?"

He nods. "That was Fischer. I have a feeling he's late for dinner."

"He'd better be! Otherwise he's going to mess up the best thing to ever happen to him. Micah is perfect for him."

"Like you're perfect for me?" Jake grabs both my hands and pulls me closer, brushing his nose against mine despite the sound of a shower turning on down the hall, reminding me we're no longer alone. "Isla, I have never loved anyone like I love you, and I would move heaven and earth to be with you. Moving a couple of hours away is nothing if it means I get to be yours. At least think about it?"

I shake my head, pressing my palm to his cheek when his face falls. "I don't have to think about it, Jake. Honestly, if my family wasn't in Diamond Springs, I would move here in a heartbeat if it meant I got to be with you."

He exhales shakily, as if he really expected me to say no to his idea. "Really?"

I press my lips to his, loving the gentle way he kisses me. "I don't want to go any longer without my husband by my side."

"Even if you married a man named Marty McFly?"

I snort a laugh and cuddle up against him again, this time with my cheek pressed against his chest. His heart beats strong and fast in my ear, and I may never get used to the sound. "I like your real name," I murmur after a few minutes. I might fail at that staying awake thing if I'm here for much longer.

Jake hums contentedly. "I like it too. But only when you use it."

"Uh." Fischer appears in the living room in a new outfit, his hair damp. That was the fastest shower I've ever seen, but he seems to have forgotten that he was in a hurry as he stares at us.

Jake chuckles. "Going somewhere fun?"

Fischer blinks several times. It's almost like he's trying to figure out if I'm real or just in his imagination. "Dinner. With Micah."

"You seem tense. But in a good way."

"Uh."

"Hi, Fischer," I say, even though I'm pretty sure Fischer doesn't know I exist. "You look nice. Whoever Micah is, she's a lucky woman."

He frowns. "What?"

"Kale has told me all about you." *Such a stupid name.*

I can feel Jake trying to hold in his laughter beneath me, though he's close to breaking. Honestly, with some of the weird things he said he's done around Fischer to try to get him to loosen up, I'm amazed he hasn't blown his cover already. Fischer thinks Jake is the strangest person in the world, and I don't blame him. He doesn't know the man I know. The man I've fallen hopelessly in love with over the last few months.

"Have a good night with Micah, Fischer," Jake says, his voice wobbly through his barely held back laughter.

Fischer blinks again, and then he clears his throat and mutters, "Right," before heading to the door.

We bust up as soon as the door closes behind him, and I rest my chin on Jake's chest. Instagram messages and occasional video chats were great, but being here with him and being able to laugh with him like this is so much better. I'm not sure I'm going to find the willpower to get on a plane the day after tomorrow.

"You would really move to Colorado?" I ask, holding my breath.

"Fischer will be fine," Jake says again, brushing my hair away from my face. "Which means there's nothing stopping me from following you to the end of the world. Or, you know, the continental US."

I snicker and lean forward to kiss him again. "I won't say no to that. My apartment is going to feel lonely anyway, and being apart from you was kind of the worst. Besides, I need a way to repay you for buying my leg from sleazy Geoff."

Jake snorts. "You really don't."

"What is that supposed to mean?"

He bites his lip to hold back his grin, though the movement just makes me want to claim that lip for myself. Curiosity keeps me away, though. "It means I broke into his security and offered to strengthen it for him. For a fee."

I gasp. "Jake Moody! I thought you weren't going to do anything illegal anymore!"

Laughing, he kisses the tip of my nose and runs his thumb across my cheek. "It's called white hat hacking, which is an unfortunate name, but it's perfectly ethical." But then he grimaces. "Except maybe in this case it was more of a grey hat situation, but I didn't steal anything, I promise. And now the guy has extra good security, so we both won."

I can't even be mad at him, considering how ridiculous the price was for my prosthesis. "As long as you promise to never do anything illegal from here on out."

"Easily. As long as I have you, I don't need anything else."

Those are big words, ones I fully intend to exploit. I may not have known this man for long, but I've never known anyone as well as I know him. I refuse to let that go. "Hey, Jake?"

"Yeah?"

"Do you want to be my husband for real so I never have to say goodbye to you?"

He grins, showing me that dimple that I love so much. "I thought you'd never ask."

And then he kisses me, his kiss promising a future that is so much brighter than anything I could have dreamed up for myself.

Also by Dana LeCheminant

A World without You
Love, Strictly Speaking

Historical Romances
The Thief and the Noble
A Twist of Christmas (part of The Holly and the Ivy anthology)
What Dreams May Come
This Above All

About the Author

Dana LeCheminant has been telling stories since she was old enough to know what stories were. After spending most of her childhood reading everything she could get her hands on, she eventually realized she could write her own books too, and since then she always has plots brewing and characters clamoring to be next to have their stories told. A lover of all things outdoors, she finds inspiration while hiking the remote Utah backcountry and cruising down rivers. Until her endless imagination runs dry, she will always have another story to tell.

Made in the USA
Middletown, DE
23 September 2023

39151098R00066